I0591045

DESPERATE DAYS

An Albre Novel, Days of My Life Series

MONTGOMERY
I-65

NEXT EXIT

Bo Hall

Desperate Days

An Albre Novel, Days of My Life Series

By: Bo Hall

Cover illustrated by: Dewayne Moss
Cover Designed & Created by: Jazzy Kitty Publishing
Logo designs by: Andre M. Saunders and Leroy Grayson

Editor: Anelda L. Attaway
Co-Editor: Bo Hall

© 2013 Bo Hall

ISBN: 978-09892656-2-1
Library of Congress Control Number: 2013941295

ACKNOWLEDGMENTS

First and foremost, I give thanks to Our Lord Jesus Christ, for forgiving me of my trespasses, as I forgive those that have trespassed against me. All things are possible through You Lord, and I give You all the praise!!!

Thanks to my daughter Alexandra, Bre', you are my everything, you are the reason I keep on keeping on. Daddy loves you so much.

Thanks Grandma Sister Ethel Fuller Hale, for taking us in after my mother's death, and teaching me how to be respectful, honest, and God fearing.

Thanks to my sibling Bryant, Libridget (Black), Latoya (Pumpkin), Marquee, Tarrence, Tamaria, Jasmine, Pat and his wife Kat for all the unconditional love and support. Bruh, you like a father, mentor, and sometimes my counselor (smile). Thanks man.

Thanks to my dad and his wife (Mr. and Mrs. Joseph Sr.), for always having my back, regardless.

Thanks to my family in Lowndes County (45), Selma, and Montgomery (The Gump) Alabama. Support your very own country boy. Shout out to KY family in Georgia and Las Vegas.

A big THANKS to my publisher, Mrs. Anelda Attaway (JazzyKitty) of Jazzy Kitty Publishing, also for the many hours of editing. Thanks for the all the help and advice on my very first project. Jazzy Kitty Publishing is doing big things.

Thanks to my family on the inside (Georgia Dept of Correction), you all know who you are because I talk to you on the daily basis asking for advice, seeking an encouraging word, or just laughing and kicking it. You all are my peers, my friends, and my enemies. I wouldn't be doing my book any justice trying to name everyone, plus my publisher said it would make my book look ghetto trying to name pookie and dem. Just playing Mrs. Attaway (smile).

My inside family stay encouraged. Remember, anything is possible with God, work on yourself as a person and respect yourself, and then everyone else will respect you. I understand the struggle, and we will get our *second chance* in either this life or the next. **Don't blow it.**

DEDICATIONS

This book is for my mother the late Mary Helen Hall (1954-1989), I love you and I miss you so so much.

R.I.P.

TABLE OF CONTENTS

TABLE OF CONTENTS

INTRODUCTION

"This is Kayla Lee, with WXYN 10 o'clock news and for our top story; the Montgomery Police Department is investigating the brutal murders and robbery of Top Knotch Jewelry. Top Knotch Jewelry is located on the Westside, on Fairview Avenue and is suspected to be a drug trade-off spot for some of the South's most notorious drug dealers. Police responded to a 911 call of a robbery at about nine pm tonight. Upon arrival, three black males and an Asian were shot to death, in what appears to be a robbery homicide. Police suspect drugs was involved, and they have yet to release the identity of the victims, pending notification to the families. However, one of the victims is believed to be the owner of the jewelry store. Police have reason to believe this was a setup for robbery. The MPD has no suspects at this time. However, a witness saw a black Mercedes Benz leaving the scene of crime, and asks that anyone with information, please call their hotline number. The MPD is not saying what was taken, and how much. We have a source close to the investigation who tells us that the estimate value of the jewelry and cash is in the millions, also an unknown amount of drugs. Investigations continue. Again, Montgomery Police Department asks anyone with any information call 1-800-STOP-CRIME or MPD at 301-288-5555. Also in the news..." LaToya turns the TV off; wondering was that Albre, who pulled the robbery at Top Knotch Jewelry. But, she knew better than to ask.

Albre gets out the shower and gets dress, and then they exit the hotel room unto their awaiting cab. At 11:45 p.m., their flight leaves.

CHAPTER 1

The Beginning of May

Albre rides down Westsouth Blvd. in his 1983 prime down Cutlass, thinking to himself how many Friday nights he has ridden this trip. Watching the people pass him in rims that cost more than his college education. He pulls over at the Texaco Gas Station to get 5 dollars in gas. Cursing the day, he can get out of Montgomery. Life is good in the "Gump." It's a city on the rise. However, it's still too slow for him after spending last summer in Las Vegas with his older brother, Supreme.

Yeah, Supreme moved out to Vegas five years ago and was doing well. Even though, Supreme has a degree in Computer Science from the University of Alabama. He decided to open up a strip club. He was doing well for himself and India, his supermodel girlfriend.

Albre gets out of the old beat down Cutlass, goes inside the store, and pays for his gas. He also buys a box of Black & Milds and a box of Swiser Blunts.

"Is that all?" asked the cashier.

"Yeah," said Albre.

He really didn't want to be bothered by the white lady. So he goes outside and starts to pump his gas. He sees his boy John; he pulls up in his 2000 Eddie Bauer Expedition.

"Yo, Albre! What's the move, man?" John hollers at him as he jumps out the truck with rims big enough to fit on a tracker trailer.

"What's happening, John? You just the person I need to see," said

Albre.

"What you 'bout to get into? Want to ride wit me?" John asked.

"Yeah, what you got planned?" Albre responded.

"You know me, just hitting a few spots," said John.

"Well, let me drop my car at my crib," said Albre.

Albre jumps in the Cutlass and waits for John to come out the store. John follows him to his house in Ridgecrest. Albre parks the car in front of his dad's house and ask John if he needs to bring his heater.

"Nah, man. We don't need to ride too dirty. I already got my 45, and all this weed," said John.

John showed Albre a Ziploc bag with a quarter pound of weed. Albre jumps into the passenger seat of his homeboy's truck, immediately plugs in his cell phone into the cigarette lighter to charge his battery. John puts the truck in drive and heads for the freeway. Albre takes out a box of blunts and began breaking one down. John gives him the weed, and he rolls a blunt. He fires it up, and then passes it to John.

"Damn, this some good weed. Is this the same weed you had last week?" Albre asked.

"Man, you know I don't sit on that shit long. This is from Rico. Rico hooked up with this nigga out of Atlanta. I tell you Rico is bigger than life!" John said.

"You I heard about some cat in Atlanta. They say he got the South on lock," said Albre.

John gets off on the exit and heads towards the Montgomery Mall. Albre's feeling good; he likes riding in John's truck. He can't wait to get his own.

"School out next week, what you gonna do?" John asked.

He pulls into the mall parking lot. Albre can feel eyes watching him and John as they get out the Expedition.

"Damn, John. I'm trying to ride like you. I'm planning on getting in the game. See how much money I can make," Albre continued, "hell, even my baby momma making more money than me."

They go into the mall, and they stopped at the store called Finish Line. John buys a pair of all white Air Force Ones. Albre purchased a Cleveland Indians baseball fitted cap. They stroll inside the mall, looking high as hell. When they got to the food court, Albre is called over by a girl in one of his classes at Alabama State University

"What's up, Tiffany?" Albre asked.

"Shit, me and my girls just out shopping," answered Tiffany. He noticed all the bags they had.

"Me and my girls plan on going to the new Club Platinum tonight. What's up with you and your boy?" Tiffany asked.

Albre introduces them, "Tiffany; this is John." John checks out Tiffany. She's 5'4", light brown skin, micro braids with beautiful hazel brown eyes. John was definitely interested.

"Oh, we will most definitely be where you all are gonna be at," replied John, elated.

Tiffany said, "Alright, we'll see you and you at the club." Tiffany winks at John before they leave. Albre and John go back outside to John's truck. Albre's cell phone rings and he answers it.

"Hello," said Albre.

"Where you at?" Shonta his baby momma asked.

"You can't talk no better than that. I'm with John," said Albre.

"I just wanted to let you know I'm going out tonight. I'm gonna drop Bre off at your grandmother's," said Shonta. *(Bre was their daughter)*.

"Yeah, yeah. It's cool," said Albre, "but check with grandma first." Then he hangs up the phone. John tells Albre they might as well swing by Gage's party. Gage lived down the street from Albre, and he was cool with that.

CHAPTER 2

Club Platinum

When Albre and John left Gage's party, it was 11:30 p.m., so they headed for Club Platinum. When they reached the club it was already packed.

"Damn, this club already packed," said Albre. This was his first time going to Club Platinum.

"I heard Big Rick brought his clientele with him when he came down from Atlanta," said John as he found a parking spot.

"You know Big Rick had a hit on his head for a 100 grand; that's why he moved to the Gump. I hope he don't think these cats in the Gump won't cash in on his head the first chance they get," said Albre while rolling a blunt.

They sat in the parking lot for about 10 minutes watching Girls Gone Wild on the TV screen in John's truck. Black pulls up in a 2000 Fleetwood. Black's music was playing loud; they heard it over the clubs music. He parks beside them; he gets out, and then jumps in the back of John's truck.

"What brings you kids out tonight?" Black asked them jokingly. Black was 40 plus and always looked out for John and Albre. Even though he was twice their age, he always had some bad hoes with him. Albre wondered what he did to keep all those bad hoes around him. It had to be the money because Black had plenty of it. He had been selling dope out of his car wash since Albre could remember.

"We figure we would get out to the new spot. I heard Club Platinum was the place to be on Friday nights," said John as he passed a blunt to Black.

Black hits the blunt and then said, "Hell, ya'll gonna miss all the action out here. I'm going in, catch ya later."

Black exits the truck, retrieves his girls from the Fleetwood and enters the club. They watch them go in as they saw this Cadillac Escalade pull up and four girls get out and go into the club. So they decided it was definitely time to make their presence known.

"I'm leaving my phone in the truck, so if we leave separate, make sure it's turned on," said Albre as they get out.

When they approached the door, John pulls out a knot of bills and pays his way in. Albre did the same, only his knot was not as big as his boy was. John went straight to the bar. Albre found a table near the back where they could watch all the action. John came back to the table struggling to carry a pint of Remy Martin, 4 Coronas, and two cups of ice.

"There goes Tiffany and her girls. Look at the way she works the floor. She moves as if she owns the space," said Albre.

"I know something else she can work," John commented.

After sitting and observing the scene, John decides he would approach Tiffany. As soon as he left, Albre sees this bad black chocolate stallion of a woman walking his way.

"Hello, how are you? Is this seat taken?" she asked, "my name is Nikki."

"Yeah, sure. Have a seat, I'm Albre," he said as he stands and move the chair so Nikki could sit down.

"You from around here 'cause I haven't seen you here before?" Nikki asked. She was looking oh-so-luscious dressed in a blue body fitting Baby Phat dress.

"Yeah, my first time at this club, I got into Alabama State," he said.

"Well, I'm from Selma; I come to Montgomery almost every weekend. My friends love this club," said Nikki.

As Albre and Nikki talks some more he finds out she goes to Wallace Community College in Selma. They talk and dance, and before Albre knows it, John is saying he's about to leave with Tiffany. He gives Albre the keys to his truck and tells him to make sure his phone is on, and that he would need him to pick him up from the Pebbler's Inn. Albre goes back and asks Nikki what was her plans after the club.

"The night is still young," she replies.

"Would you like to grab a bite to eat?" Albre asked Nikki then continued, "hell the club closes at three. It's two now."

"Sure, let me tell my girls so they'll know I'm going," said Nikki as she walks away. When Nikki returns they leave the club.

"This is your truck?" Nikki asked.

"Nah, this is my partner's truck, he has so many toys, some he don't even play wit," explains Albre.

"The Waffle House is right up the street. Is that cool?" Albre asked.

"Yeah, I'm starved," said Nikki.

When they ate, Albre asked Nikki did she want to get a room. She agreed, so they checked into the Ramada Inn. Albre noticed how low his money was, so something had to give. He thinks as they go into the room. Nikki had a banging body, and Albre enjoyed himself. Not really into foreplay because he just met her. But all the same, Nikki had some good pussy. His phone rings, and he noticed it was John.

"Come get me," said John.

"Aight, I'm on the way. Give me about 10 minutes," said Albre.

He tells Nikki to get dress so they can pick up John, and then he can take her home. After they dropped Nikki off at her apartment in Selma, it was dawn. So he let John drive back to the Gump.

CHAPTER 3

School Ended...Now Get Money

School ended the last week in May. Albre was elated not to have to go to class. Now he could concentrate on getting some money. He was tired of being broke and driving that raggedy ass Cutlass. His first step would be to get money, and then holler at John about purchasing some dope. He has not seen him since that night at Club Platinum.

Monday morning Albre gets up; he is glad that he didn't have to return to the Alabama State until August. In the meantime, he called John.

"Hello," said John as he answers on the first ring.

"Say, John, I need to rap wit you. So stop by my dad's house," said Albre as he sits in the living room rolling up a blunt. He hasn't even ate yet.

"I'll swing by on my way to the African Shop. In about an hour," said John.

"Aight," he said and hangs up the phone.

He fired up his first blunt of the day. Getting his mind right was a daily ritual; every morning before class, and sometimes before breakfast. However, school was out, so he decided he would call his dad at work and hit him up for some money.

"Dad," said Albre as he speaks into the cordless phone.

Then his dad said to him, "Hey, son, what's up?" His father, Melvin, was the director of Housing Division for the city of Montgomery.

"Dad, I need to borrow some money. Could I come by and pick it up?"

Albre asked his dad.

Then his dad replied to him and asked, "How much you need, son?"

He didn't sound pleased that Albre wanted more money. After all, he was paying for his son's college education and living expenses.

"About 12 hundred, Dad. I promise to pay it back," said Albre as he pleads with his father.

His father said to him in a stern voice, "I'm gonna give you the money. But you need to find a job, Albre. I mean it!"

"I'm on my way out there," said Albre as he hangs up the phone.

He goes outside to check the oil and water in his car. His father taught him that if he kept up his car's maintenance it would last longer. After checking the fluids, he gets in the Cutlass and heads straight to his dad's office. Hoping John does not come by while he's gone. Albre hated going to his dad's office in the summer. School was out so kids were everywhere. His dad's office was in one of the roughest project in the Gump Riverside. When he pulled up at the office, his dad is outside. He was talking to a guy named Roy. Roy is a maintenance man in Riverside, and he has been working for his father for three years. Albre had met him a number of times.

"Hey, Dad, Roy, how's it going?" Albre asked as he walks up the sidewalk.

"I'm okay. Your dad tells me you looking for a job. I sure could use some help around here for the summer," said Roy to Albre.

"I'll think about it," said Albre not trying to get distracted from his plans of selling dope. His father finishes talking to Roy. He turns and leads Albre into his office.

His office is in the garage of the Riverside maintenance shop. It's pretty big compared to the size of other projects maintenance shops. When they get in the office Albre notices Mrs. Meadows, his father's secretary, is not in the corner that he remembers sleeping on, on several occasions during his summer breaks when he was in junior high. Back then, he noticed that his father had an easy job. He spent most of his time in his office doing paperwork, watching TV, and on the phone with Headquarters. He would make occasional rounds to different projecthousings under housing division. His dad sits in his old leather chair behind his old wood desk, and pulls 12 hundred dollars out of his wallet, which is typical.

Albre picks up the money and said, "Dad, I promise I'll look for a job and I'll pay you back."

"Son, I just want you to do the right thing. Stay out of those streets. I've worked hard to see that you had a decent life and put you in that college you're attending. You know I love you, and I'll help you when I can as long as you do the right thing," said his dad.

"I love you, too. Thanks, Pop," said Albre. Then he was up and out the door; he loved his dad, but wasn't in the mood for a lecture.

When Albre turns on to Doris Street, where him and his dad lives; he notices John 69 cocaine-white Impala with the 22-inch chrome rims, parked in front of his house. At the same time that he turns on to the street, his phone rings, and the caller ID identifies the caller as John. He doesn't answers it as he pulls in his drive way. Albre gets out his car and gets in John's Impala.

"What's up, folk?" John asked Albre as he gets in.

"I'm good, man. I need to cop an ounce of that hard. I know you don't fuck wit the shit, but I figure you could turn me on to Rico. I'll get this junkie that braids my hair, out in Smiley Court. She told me I could set-up a shop in her place," Albre tells John.

"Aight, let me call Rico and tell him we coming by," said John as he dials a number in his phone. Albre burst down a blunt and John gives him a bag of what looks like some "Hydro." Albre rolls the blunt, John gets off the phone with Rico.

"Rico said to meet him at the spot in Washington Park. But first I got to go to the African Shop and buy this new Luke Freak Feast DVD. The one he made for spring break in Cancun, Mexico," said John as he turns onto Mobile highway.

When they pulled up at the African Shop, *(a black-owned record store that sells everything from CDs to drug paraphernalia)* John goes in while Albre sits in the car and smokes the blunt. He was somewhat nervous, even though he has seen Rico. He has never had the privilege to hold a conversation with him. John comes out the record store with two DVDs, not only Luke Freak Feast DVD but Girls Gone Wild Doggy Style featuring Snoop Dogg. They head towards Washington Park. Washington Park is a typical black neighborhood. When they get to the street, Rico has his trap located. Albre notices the street look like something out of *"Boyz N Da Hood"*. When they pulled up in front, there a money-green Oldsmobile Cutlass, with 20-inch chrome rims. A black on black chromed out '94 Tahoe sitting on 22". He doesn't see Rico 2000 candy apple red Mercedes E-320. But he knows Rico has more than one car. Albre and John gets out and go to the door. The door looks like it's made out of metal. Probably to keep the police from kicking it in, also to keep the stickup boys out.

When they get to the door, this junkie looking guy opens it. When they entered the living room, four guys playing a PlayStation 2, all smoking their own blunt. The house is filthy, but that's to be expected in a setup like this. John pushes to the back bedroom, Albre follows. John knocks on the door, Rico peaks his head out and let them in the room, and then closes the door behind them. There's not a bed in the room, instead there's a round table loaded with what got to be at least 2 kilos. Albre sees an AK assault rifle standing up in the corner. In one of the chairs is a digital scale the size of a shoebox. Albre realizes he doesn't want to be in this house no longer than he has to.

"John tells me you go to the Alabama State and that you want to start a set-up in Smiley Court. That's a nice spot, I don't have anyone out there, yet," said Rico. He passes John a blunt that smelled like laced cocaine.

"Yeah, I got this nice spot out there, should be good for making money. Plus, I know a couple people out there. I want to buy an ounce," said Albre taking the blunt from John.

After he hit it, he could taste the cocaine on his tongue. He has smoked laced blunts before. They called them "Platinum Blunts."

"I tell you what since I just got this in. I'm gonna let you have 84 grams for twelve hundred. I usually sell it for 750 an ounce," Rico said.

Albre did the math in his head, that was three ounces and by the color of it, it's got to be 60 percent pure. Hell, he could step on it and get 5 ounces, easily.

"I got eleven fifty," he tells Rico with a grin on his face.

Rico smiles and says to him, "See, I like you already, kid. I'm doing this because you're John folks, so you're my folks; and I know you're gonna come back and fuck with me."

He takes a measuring scoop, puts five scoops in a Ziploc bag. Then he places the bag on a digital scale. Albre looked at it and its 62 grams. Rico keeps adding until the scale reads 84 grams. Then he gives the bag to Albre, Albre gives him the money.

"You know how to cook that up, Albre?" Rico asked as he takes the money and sticks it in his pocket.

He tells Rico, "Yeah, I got someone to show me how to cook it up."

"Well, make sure you step on it. If you do it right, you should get 5 ounces, anything more will mess up that dope," said Rico.

Albre tells him he appreciated it and he will most definitely be back to holla at him. John tells Rico he gonna drop Albre off and he'll be back.

When they get into the car, John tells Albre that Rico must like him because he gave him the hook-up. John tells Albre to be careful as he drives him back home, and to make sure he keeps his piece close by.

They pulled up in front of Albre house. Albre tells John thanks, and he would get up with him later.

Albre tells, "Man, I got you later."

"Don't worry about it, just holla at me when you see 'Better Day'," said John. As he said that to him, he pulls off.

CHAPTER 4

Better Days

Albre calls his baby momma, Shonta to tell her he would drop by tonight to see his daughter, Bre. She tells him that they will be at her mom's house in Woodley Park, and that Bre has been asking about him. Albre hasn't seen his daughter in two days, because he has been running with the last days of school. Bre is three years old, cute and very hyperactive. Shonta names her after Albre.

When he hangs up the phone, he goes down to Gage house, who stays two streets over on Gaston Avenue. He has known Gage for about four years, ever since his dad move on Doris Street in Ridge Crest. Gage is in the Army Reserve. But he's a freelance producer, and has a bootleg studio in his house. He has some of the hardest DJ equipment around, and a top of the line computer. He was supposed to deploy to Iraq last month, and now he is AWOL.

When Albre reaches Gage's house, he sees Gage's '90 Buick LeSable in the driveway. When he gets to the door, he can see that it's open. He just goes in knowing Gage is at the computer dropping beats.

"What's up, Gage?" Albre asked.

"Damn, you scared the shit out of me," said Gage. Albre heard the beat that Gage was working on.

"You're getting better, Gage. You want to ride with me out to Smiley Court?" Albre asked.

"Nah, I got to pick up Mom Duke up from work in a while," said Gage as he turns the computer off after saving his latest beat.

"Well, when you handle your business, hit me on the hip. I got to go out here and set up shop in Smiley Court," said Albre as he looks at Gage and he leads him in the living room.

"I got to go to the bank, also," said Gage to Albre.

"Well, could you give me a ride? I don't want to be seen out there, yet," said Albre.

On their way to Smiley Court, Albre tells him about his plans to set-up shop at Cint's apartment, and how he needs him to sit with him for a couple of days to make sure everything was cool.

Gage drops him off at Cint's apartment in Smiley Court, and tells him he would be back in about two hours. Albre tells him to bring back a box of blunts and a box of Black and Milds. Albre tucks his Smith & Wesson .380 in the back of his pants before getting out the car. Albre knocks on the apartment door. Good thing Cint's apartment is downstairs. He knows everyone in Cint's apartment building because he's been there to let Cint braid his hair. Cint is his dad's ex-girlfriend's sister. He has known her ever since they moved to Montgomery when he was seven years old and she would braid hair no matter how short it was. If her fingers could catch it, then she could braid it. She kept a clean crib, besides from all the traffic because she had been smoking dope for years. She still looked decent, thick brown-skinned woman with good legs, nice ass, and big tits. You could tell she was a smoker by her face. Her face was all-thin and lips all black with brown dope-smoking teeth. Cint used to be this big dope dealer name "Chi" ole lady. Then she started smoking dope, messing with this dyke hoe named Jean. Therefore, "Chi" started pimping her and Jean until he had no more use for her. Cint opened the door, looking like she's just woke up.

"Damn, you ain't up yet. It's four o'clock," said Albre pushing pass her into the apartment. There are beer bottles and cans on the floor, ashes everywhere. He could tell she has been up all night smoking.

"What, I just braided your hair Friday. It's Monday, I know you don't need it braided again," said Cint.

"No, as a matter of fact, I need you to step on this and show me how to cook it up," said Albre. He pulls out a Ziploc bag with three ounces of cocaine. He watches, as her eyes get all big.

"Boy, lock that door while I go wash my face; and don't answer it for nobody," said Cint as she went to the bathroom.

Albre locked the door and tells Cint that he has decided to take her up on her offer about setting up shop at her apartment. He tells her he will pay the bills and keep her straight. But she had to put word out the candy shop is open.

Cint finished washing her face and came back to join Albre. Albre had laid the dope and his .380 on the table in the kitchen. He was rolling a blunt. He thought about lacing it with powder, and then decided not. He had to stay focused and watch Cint step on the dope and cook it up. Cint licks the bag of dope and sticks her finger in it to taste it.

"Damn, where you get this shit? Hell, yeah! We got to step on this. If we sell this shit you might kill these J's around here," said Cint with her face contorted as if she had been sucking on a cry baby candy ball.

"You got something to cut this with?" Albre asked her.

"Of course, I do. You know I used to cut dope for Chi back in the days. I was stepping on dope before you was steppin'," she said and smiled.

"You got a scale?" Cint asked.

"I knew I forgot something," said Albre remembering he left his digital scale at his dad's house.

"Know you ain't a dope dealer if you forget the scale, that's the most important thing. I'll go around to Jungle Baby's house and borrow his scale," she said and was out the apartment via back door. Albre got up from the kitchen table and lock the door back. He fired up his blunt.

Jungle Baby sold mad weed over on the backside of Smiley Court. Albre went to thinking that things might just go alright. However, he had to worry about the Narcos and the stickup boys. The Narcos is Montgomery Police Department Drug Task Force, and they are more like terrorists with their ruthless apprehension tactics.

Albre had hunger pains hit his stomach, and he realized he hadn't eaten all morning. So he calls Gage and tells him to stop by Joe's burgers and get him one of Joe's cheese burgers. Joe was this small restaurant on the Westside and was famous for his burgers, which is a pound of hamburger meat, and saucers sized buns, etc. His mouth watered just thinking about it.

Cint knocked at the door. Albre got his .380 automatic and peeped through the peephole.

"Jungle Baby wanted to know why I needed a scale. I told him you were over here and he said to tell you to stop by," she said sounding as if she had ran back and was out of breath. He locked the door back. Cint placed the scale on the table, gets a big bowl and some baking soda out of the cabinet. Albre watches as she mixes the baking soda with about half of the cocaine out the Ziploc. She whips it up real good. Albre looks at it and he can tell that it has turned a beige color. Cint takes a pot and heat some water until it boils. Cint takes a glass jar in which she has added the step on cocaine and place it inside the boiling hot water. Albre watches as the substance begin to cook. Once Cint was satisfied, she took it out and placed it in a pan to let it dry. Albre's amazed at how it looks soft like a piece of butter. Cint sets it to the side, let it dry, and starts on the other dope. After repeating the same process, both batches were drying. Albre smoked another blunt with Cint. Cint tells him he should get five ounces of some good hard. Albre seemed surprised at making crack cocaine. Cint tells Albre when it dries she will taste it, and then hit the block to put word out. But he shouldn't expect, with it being Monday and end of the month. But the first was Friday. By then word would be out and they would be in business.

Albre hears music coming from outside Three Six Mafia is playing. Then he looks out the window to find Gage. He hears, "Who running, ump, ump, ump..." Then Gage parks his car and comes in with a big bag. Albre was hungry so he ate his Joe burger while Gage rolled a blunt.

The dope had finally dried; he weighted it up at 133 grams, seven grams short of five ounces. Cint tastes the dope, Albre and Gage watch.

"Dis da shit." Cint said through the smoke. She was exhaling. Albre cared not to small the shit. But hell, he could deal with it until Better Days.

CHAPTER 5

The Month of June

June first came quick and Albre had been slanging out of Cint apartment for five days now. But everything started out slow, Cint trying to smoke everything in sight. Albre has been there from sun up to sun down every day and he had made $3,200. Gage has been coming back and forth. But he could tell it was the first of the month because everybody was dressed in their best clothes. He had already made $800 and it's only one o'clock. He spent time with his daughter last night and had to put up with Shonta asking all types of questions about what he was doing in Smiley Court. He gave her two hundred dollars to shut her mouth up and for her to buy Bre some clothes. He didn't care what she did with the rest.

He still had to call John to go re-up with Rico. Even though he had a little more than two ounces left. John came and picked him up. Albre left about ten twenties with Cint.

Albre bought about three more ounces. But the only love Rico showed him this time were letting him cop them for five hundred a piece, which was better than what everyone else was doing. An ounce in the Gump went for eight hundred easily. But he knew Rico was letting him buy them for the five, because he wanted him to keep coming back.

When John dropped him back off in Smiley Court at Cint's apartment, Gage was waiting on him. Albre went into the apartment gave Gage the dope to sell while he watched Cint step on and cook the new batch. Cint gave him $100 for the five of ten twenties she sold while he was away.

Albre tell her to keep it, go pay the light bill, then gave her $100 more after she finished cooking the dope. This time she got exactly five ounces.

"Take that money and my car. Go pamper yourself and get stuff for the house," said Albre. He knows Cint just got her check and her food stamps would come through on the fifteenth of the month.

"Ya'll need anything?" Cint asked as she was leaving out the apartment.

"Some more bags, a box of blunts, and a case of coronas," barked Albre. He had enough Black & Mild cigars and some Hennessy left over from last night.

"And some ice," said Gage watching Cint as she backs Albre's primed down Cutlass out of the driveway.

"You trust her with your car?" Gage asked, not knowing Albre and Cint's history.

"Hell yeah, she's good people. Besides, we're at her crib, she trusts us to leave us here," said Albre. Then realizing how ridiculous he sounded because nothing in Cint apartment was really worth any value, not as of yet, anyway.

As they sat listening to the radio with the TV on; traffic came and left. Albre served some junkies he didn't know and some he hasn't seen in years. They all told him he had some of the best dope on the Southside. Smiley Court was Southwest Montgomery, but everyone considers it the Southside. Albre sold the other two ounces before Cint came back and made $5,800 with the three thousands he already had. He decides it was time to go drop off some money.

"Say, Gage, let me use your car to go around the corner and buy some weed from Jungle Baby. I need to stop by the house, too," he said.

Gage gave him the keys to the Buick LaSable and started back talking on his phone. Albre didn't really like driving Gage's car. Gage was a Gangsta Disciple and he knows Gage has been in shootouts and confrontations lately, probably in his game car. Albre pulls up in front of Jungle Baby's apartment and goes in.

"What's up, Albre? I heard you got it sewed up on the front side. Glad you ain't selling weed. I would hate to have to see about you," Jungle Baby said while smiling showing a mouthful of gold teeth. He had dreads so you would think he was a Rasta boy, if it wasn't for the Gump Southern accent.

Albre puts Jungle Baby up on the events of the last week. Jungle Baby's crib was just like every other dope trap in the Gump. House full of young niggas, every one of them had two or more gold teeth and lips black as if they had been smoking for decades.

"Yeah, man. I'm trying to get the money. But what you got for me? I need an ounce of Hydro," said Albre.

"I got you, my nigga," Jungle Baby tells Albre and puts a Ziploc bag full of weed on a scale in the kitchen.

Albre sees that it weigh 28 grams so he gives Jungle Baby four hundred dollars and tells him he has to push on. When Albre gets in Gage's car, he sees the pigs parked down the block, so he puts the weed in his lap in case he has to throw it out the window.

Albre drives to his dad's house on Doris Street, and sees that his dad isn't home yet. So he jumps out the car to go put the five thousand dollars in the house. He put the money in a pair of jeans in his closet. He checks the caller ID to see if his baby momma, Shonta called. Her number wasn't on it.

CHAPTER 6

Cint's Apartment in Smiley Court

Once Albre gets back to Cint's apartment in Smiley Court, he sees junkies coming out the apartment, so he gets out and locks the doors to Gage's car. He sees Cint pulling in the parking lot behind Gage's car. She gets out carrying all kinds of bags.

"Help me with these bags, boy," Cint demands. He goes and helps her with the bag. When inside the apartment, Gage tells him how he was holding things down while he was out. Then hands him some money for the dope he sold while Albre was away.

"You brought any razors?" Albre asked.

Cint throws a pack of single edge razors on the table, and tells him to cut her a piece of dope. She looks impatience. Albre cut her a nice fifty piece. Then starts rolling himself a blunt. Gage takes the razor and starts cutting some fifty pieces and then some twenty pieces. It's going to be a long weekend.

Albre fires up the blunt, walks outside, and stands by the front door. Gage joins him, leaving Cint to her dope. Outside Albre can see that people are hanging on the block. BBQ grills are smoking. Middle age folks sitting on their front porches with coolers nearby engaged in conversation, drinking their beers and spirits. Albre is approached by a white guy. He didn't see where he came from. He appeared to be in his forties, blond hair cropped short, sunburned skin, wearing denim jeans and a Newport Pleasure T-shirt. The construction worker type that has been in the sun too long. He looked like he had a monkey on his back. Oh yeah, a crack head.

"Let me get two twenties," said the white guy. Albre doesn't talk, he steps back inside the apartment as not to be seen selling dope on camera, if one was recording. He gives the junkie the dope, and then counts the money. The white junkie was short a dollar short. Albre excuse him and watches him walk away.

"Damn, it's four o'clock. I got to go pick up my mom," Gage tells him while talking on the phone, presumably his mom.

"I'll be back in about an hour," said Gage as he walks to his car.

It seem as soon as Gage left, traffic picks up. Albre found himself opening the door to the apartment every other minute. Twenties, fifties, and a couple of hundred-dollar pieces were all he sold. Someone would come by every now and then and bought dimes. He knew those people would be back all night. Thinking that by spending ten dollars at a time, they got more crack. When in actuality they were only cheating themselves. Albre did not complain for it was the first of the month. Cint was back there shut up in her room. Albre could picture her looking on the floor for dope. Picking up trash, thinking it was crack while knowing damn well she ain't dropped a crump. They all the same once they get that first hit. Then Albre began to feel bad about selling crack to his own people. Some of the people he sold to help raised him growing up in Victor Tulane Apartments, when he first moved to Montgomery. But that guilty conscious passed quickly, when he thought about leaving the Gump going somewhere more exciting.

"Hello," Albre answers his cell phone.

"Come outside, I'm turning the corner," said John on the phone.

Albre hangs up and steps outside to see John pulls up in front of the apartment.

"Damn, I hear you jumpin' hard," said John with a grin on his face.

"Getting to the money, so I can ride like you, my nigga," said Albre.

"What's up? What you getting into tonight?" John asked. "I know you want to hit Club Platinum tonight."

"Nah, I'm on the grind all night. You got some powder? My dumb ass cooked all mine up," said Albre.

"Yeah, I got cha. You ever talk to that broad you met at the club last time?" John asked him.

"I talked to Nikki twice. I ain't going all the way to Selma. I told her to hit me when she in the Gump," said Albre. John and Albre walked in the apartment where John gives Albre an 8-ball.

"That's str-8," said John.

"Yeah, I'm gonna be up all night," said Albre as he goes to make a quick sell.

"You know Cash that owns Top Knotch Jewelry? He hollered at me today. He told me to stop by and he said he has all I need," said John to Albre.

"So you gonna fuck with him?" Albre asked.

"Yeah, if his price is right, because Rico is hot right now with the Feds," said John.

John tells him that he was going to holla at Cash tomorrow. Albre tells John he was going to hit him up later. John gave him some daps and leaves.

When John leaves, Cint comes out her room and her eyes are all big like she has been spooked by a ghost. She gives Albre a hundred dollars for some more dope, and then she leaves and goes around the block. When Gage returns it was dark outside so Albre's happy that he's back. They sat around drinking Coronas and smoking Platinum blunts and Albre makes more money than he ever seen.

CHAPTER 7

August...Time to Start a New Semester

So the days and months passed by just like that when August came around and it was time for Albre to start a new semester at the Alabama State.

Him and Gage goes out and buy twin '89 Chevy Suburban, the square body ones. Albre's was in better shape than Gage when they first got them. Albre drives his Cutlass to school on his first day, back in class. He had gotten his car painted mint green with the interior upholstered in tan and brown and has also got a 305 small block in it with the floor master that made it sound heavy.

Albre felt real larger than life; pulling up at the Alabama State in his Cutlass sitting on 20' Neptunes rims. He had a new wardrode full of expensive clothes. He purchased only the latest urban wear. He had started letting his hair lock, so now he was sporting dreads.

Even though Albre made a lot of money that summer, he was determined to get his Major in Political Science and undermajor in marketing and management. He wanted to start a management consulting company. While Albre sat in class, he was confident in knowing Gage was holding the trap down. When Albre left school his first day, he noticed all the attention he was getting.

"Damn, it felt good to have money," he thought.

He picks up his daughter Bre from daycare and takes her to McDonalds to get a Happy Meal.

"Daddy, Daddy, Daddy, can I have a Happy Meal?" his daughter said as they were pulling up at McDonalds.

"Yeah, and you can have an ice cream, too. Once you eat your hamburger," said Albre to his daughter.

The drive-thru was packed, so they got out and went in. Albre eats at this McDonalds regularly because it's on Fairview close to his dad's house. His neighbor Meka works here, so he gets in Meka's line because she likes Albre and adores Bre. Maybe he can pay for Bre's Happy Meal and get his for free.

"What's up, Meka? You're looking good," said Albre.

"Hey, Albre, oh, hey Bre. How you doing?" Meka said to Bre.

"Fine," said Bre like a grown woman.

Albre orders Bre's Happy Meal and like usual, Meka asked him what he would like. He tells her a double Quarter Pounder with cheese and extra onions, and two ice creams mike shakes. She charges him only $1.99 for Bre's Happy Meal.

"Thanks, Meka," said Albre.

"Thank you, Meka," said Bre as she marks her father holding her Happy Meal.

"It's a toy inside," Meka tells Bre.

"Albre, why don't I see you at home that much?" Meka asked Albre.

"I'll be in Smiley Court most of the time," said Albre.

"You got some girl out there?" Meka asked.

"No, trappin'," said Albre.

"Well, holla at me sometimes Albre," said Meka as they were leaving out the door.

Albre remembers the time he almost got caught sneaking out Meka's window. Meka's mom, Mrs. Parker, knew something was going on between her daughter and Albre but Meka's dad was the one that almost caught him sneaking out Meka's window. Meka got into trouble with her parents. She stayed solid, because she didn't tell on Albre.

After Albre drops his daughter off at Shonta's house, Bre's grandmothers, he heads to Smiley Court to get on the grind. When he gets to Smiley Court, traffic is heavy because school is just getting out.

Albre pulls up at Cint's apartment. Gage is sitting on the porch talking on his phone. Albre notices this girl that stays two buildings down. Her name is LaToya and he's been wanting to catch up with her so he could spit game at her. Right now, she's standing on her porch talking to another girl that stays in tis housing projects. Gage catches him staring.

"What you looking at?" Gage asked as she was walking up to Albre. Once he notices the girl Albre was looking at she said, "Oh."

"How did it go today?" Albre asked Gage.

"Slow, but I brought some rims for the 'Burban," said Gage. He tells Albre he gave this dude an ounce for some 22" Daytons.

"Word, where they at?" asked Albre. Gage shows him the rims, he had stored in the extra bedroom of Cint's apartment.

"Those phat," said Albre examining the rims.

Albre goes into the living room and rolls up a blunt. Gage brings him a Corona. Albre takes his dope out and starts cutting it up. These days he and Gage have been buying dope together. But they never buy more than five ounces at a time, and they always buy it soft so they can cook it up themselves. Gage pockets are as fat as his, now. Albre didn't mind Gage getting money with him, because he knows Gage had his back. He learned from his brother, that loyalty goes a long way, Gage was older than him. Gage both respected and feared him; he knew Albre was trained to go, and wouldn't think twice about killing someone who crossed him. Behind that pretty boy face, Albre didn't have a conscious.

About when Albre was 16 years old, word was that Albre killed two niggers in Michigan for his brother, and made away with a lot of weed. Albre has always been the go to man, because his dad took him hunting when he was younger. Before his dad did that bid in prison. Gage has seen Albre in action and knew Albre could shoot a moving target, at least, a hundred yards with a high-powered rifle.

CHAPTER 8

Albre at Cint's Apartmennt

Albre pulls up at Cint's apartment in Smiley Court. He parks his '89 Chevy Suburban behind Gage's 89' Chevy Suburban. They both had just left from picking their trucks up from the paint shop. Lee at Stupid Auto Body had put his spray down again on the Suburbans'. Stupid Auto Body Shop was the most in demand car shop on the Eastside of the Mississippi river. He had painted Gage's truck smoke gray, and Albre had his painted a butterscotch candy. Albre is just pulling up because he had to stop by Chuck's Tire and Rim shop to get his 22"inch Sprewells put on.

Albre notices that Gage's Suburban looks wet with them 22" Dayton. He let all the windows down in his truck and gets out. The only seat in the truck is the driver seat. Because he has them being upholstered, and he had to drop the truck off tomorrow to get the rest of his interior beige and four TVs and three 12" woofers put in. Cint greets Albre at the door, looking like she's losing weight by the minute. She still had all her good features intact. He should know he has gotten his dick sucked by her numerous times.

"Hey, Albre, your truck looks good. What happen to yall seats?" Cint asked.

"I took 'em out. I like to ride solo," he laughs, pushing his way in the apartments. Gage is playing PlayStation 2 on Cint's TV.

Albre sat down and checked his pager to see who called because he had left it there. He noticed that Gage is playing Madden Football, so he asked to play. But first, he rolls a blunt while Gage starts the game over. Him and Gage sit around and smoke blunt after blunt while playing the PlayStation for about two hours when John pulls up in a Ford Taurus rental car.

"What's good, Albre, Gage?" John asked as he gives Cint a Newport cigarette.

Albre said, "Chillin'."

"Nothin'," added Gage.

Then John tells them, "Yeah, Albre, you know the Feds knocked Rico today, caught him leaving a storage place with two bricks."

"What?" Albre commented, while not taking his eyes off the game. He's beating Gage by a touchdown. But Gage has the ball and he's inside touchdown range.

"They had the storage place under surveillance. He tried to run hot. They had him blocked in," John continues to tell them while they nodded their heads in understanding, eyes glued on the TV, "and the Feds stopped one of Peef distribution trucks between Atlanta and Phoenix City, Alabama. That mutha fucka was loaded with 120 bricks and one and a half tons of weed." John fired up one of his platinum blunts. You can tell by the smell of it.

"Don't Peef deliver to the Department of Corrections?" Gage asked.

"Yeah, not only in Alabama but every prison system in the South," confirms John.

"Damn, that was sweet diversion," said Albre placing the PlayStation controller on the table because he just beat Gage's Atlanta Falcons by a field goal.

John passed Gage the blunt. Now, Cint's playing in Albre's hair, telling him he needs to get his new growth twisted. Albre tells her tomorrow. John tells Albre he needs him to ride with him. Albre gives Cint two twenties before he leaves.

Once in the rental, car John asked Albre if he has his pistol. Albre smiles and show him this black Glock nine millimeter. Albre don't go too many places without his sixteen rounds, one in the chamber Glock nine.

"What's up, John? What's the move?" Albre asked.

John fills him in on the way to old Selma Highway. It's down the back way to Lowndes County. John tells him that this cat named Head has been setting niggas up, and he believed that he blowed the whistle on Rico, so they were going to teach him a lesson. Albre knows Head but he could care less about Rico. However, John is his best friend, so he has to ride; and everybody knows that today it's Rico, but a snitch is a snitch. Next time he gets in trouble, he might blow the whistle on John or even Albre.

When they make it to Old Selma Highway, the sun had gone down so it is dark outside. John tells him that Head is probably in there with this bitch name Lil' Bit. Lil' Bit was this jay hoe. But if anybody else is in there, just contain them while he got the dope and the money. But he was gone burn Head and anyone else if they trys something stupid.

They parked down the street at an abandon house; it was about two houses down from the corner. It had all kinds of bushes grew up around the house and drive way. So John backed the Taurus beside the abandoned house, facing the road. So they can make a clean get away. It's not too often many police ride down this particular way. It's the sheriff's district anyway.

John gives Albre a black ski mask. Albre takes off his Sean John shirt, so now him and John are both identical with black t-shirts and jeans. Albre put one in the chamber and takes the Glock off safety. John has a .40 caliber. They go around the back of the abandoned house, because none of the houses is fenced in. John leads the way to the back of Head's house. They check out the back, but go to the front door. John knocks once when he hears footsteps. Albre kicks the door in and it gave instantly. They had already checked the lock so Albre knew it would give; most dope dealers don't have the sense to upgrade their locks.

When the door gave, John leads into the house. He sees Head running to the back of the house, Albre grabs Lil' Bit who is standing in the doorway of the kitchen screaming and forced her to the floor.

"Who else is here, bitch?" Albre said opening the door to one of the two bedrooms in the house.

Albre remembers the walls to the third bedroom has been torn down to make the living room bigger. He hears two shots coming out the other bedroom where John was with Head. John came flying out the back room with a backpack. Albre tore it down behind John. They both ran as if the Grim Reaper was behind them. John throws Albre the keys. He fumbles with the ignition when John jumps in and slams the door. They get halfway down Old Selma Highway. They take off their ski masks. John tells him to go the back way to Riverside. When they got ready to cross Camp Creek Bridge. John tosses the .40 Caliber over the bridge into the creek.

Albre drops John off at his truck in Riverside. John follows him to King Hill where he wiped the Taurus clean of fingerprints. He parks it near a crack house and leaves the key in the ignition. He jumps in the truck with John. Someone is sure to steal the Taurus and take it to a chop shop or probably get caught joy-riding in it. John tells him on the way back to Smiley Court that everything is straight. He could keep all the drugs they got from Head. He said it should be three ounces of crack and three pounds of Hydro weed, and some cash, but get of the backpack like Albre needed to be told that.

They stopped at Race Trac Gas Station where John filled the Expedition with gas. Albre purchased a 12-pack of MGD, a box of blunts, five boxes of Black & Mild, and a pack of cigarettes for Cint. He throws the backpack away before they leave the gas station, and he puts the drugs with the beer. When they get back to Smiley Court, it's dark. Albre's truck just as he left it. So he let the windows up and locks the doors. As he was doing this, he sees Gage peeping out the blinds to let Albre know he was on point. Gage was talking on the phone while Cint braided his hair when they walked in.

"Where you been?" Gage asked, "Shonta came by and said your not answering your phone and your pager's here, so call that girl and see what it is she wants."

Albre checks his phone and sure enough, the battery is dead. Those Nokia phone batteries dies too quick. He plugs his phone up to Gage's adapter and calls Shonta on John's cell phone. John has a Motorola Star Trac phone.

"Where ya trippin' ass been? You turn ya phone off so I can't call. You must been wit sum bitch," Shonta shouts in his ear. He smiles, same ole Shonta.

"Damn, girl. Chill out. I been with John and my phone went dead," said Albre as he tries to calm his baby momma down.

"What's up? Everything alright?" he asked.

"Oh, I wanted to ask you to pick Bre up tomorrow from daycare. I got a job interview at Baptist Hospital," said Shonta.

"Yeah, I'll pick up Bre. Why didn't you just leave a message on my phone, Shonta?" he asked.

"Because I wanted to make sure you got the message. I don't want my baby stuck at that daycare, because you didn't get my message," said Shonta.

"Whatever," said Albre

"Whatever my ass," said Shonta as she changes her tone, sounding more seductive, "You coming by tonight? Bre wants to see you."

Albre knows this routine. Shonta's horny and she wants him to hit that thang. So he made her mad because he can.

"Nah, I got plans, but kiss Bre for me, okay," said Albre and hung up the phone before Shonta really had a chance to respond. He's thinking to himself he's a dirty ass nigga.

CHAPTER 9

Albre, John, and Gage

Albre, John, and Gage stayed up drinking beer, and smoking 'Dro. They even snorted some powder. John and Gage basically snorted the powder. Albre just snorted once or twice, and laced his blunts with it. They had sent Cint to the store to get some more beer. Albre don't know why John let Cint take his Expedition, high as she was.

Cint made it back safely with a case of MGD, and some fresh Newports. John gave Cint some dope and watched her go over the table and fixes her shooter up.

Gage walks out to his truck and brings a flick and pops in the VCR. Gage had bought the VCR for Cint last week from this girl that boost everything. They sit down and watch fuck tapes. There's two black chicks on with this white guy. The black woman with the big tits is sucking the white dude's dick. He had a nice size dick to be a white man. The one with the pretty face bounced up and down on the white guy's face, and she's making all kinds of moaning noises. Albre watches Cint sucks on her shooter, like she sucking on a glass dick, and she want to get all the cum out of it.

"Give me another piece of your dope, John, your dope different from Albre," said Cint.

John had told Albre earlier that he had got some dope from Cash. It was supposed to be a better grade, and Albre could tell it was by the look in Cint's eyes.

"Suck this dick!" John said while pulling of his pants.

"Why you have to go through this John? You gonna blow my high," cries Cint.

"What you gonna do?" John asked her. Cint walks around the table and pull John dick out and start sucking on it like she really doesn't want to. Albre gets up and locks the dead bolts locks, which he already had the bottom lock on but traffic had slowed down.

Albre has been through this with his friends and different women many times. John was always trying to turn a woman out. He was the freak of the crew. There's at least one in every crew. He was Albre's boy and he loved that crazy young nigga. He would go to war with John at his side. They had been through a lot of shit together, and John has helped him out with money more times than once.

The fuck tape had a change of scene. It was now showing two black girls who looked about sixteen, and two black guys. They were all in the living room. The tall black guy with the little ass had the young black girl with the big dick-sucking lips bend over the sofa. While he fucks her from behind, standing up. The other black guy, the swole one, was sitting on the loveseat. The older black girl rode his dick. She's making all kinds of fuck faces. The cameraman was doing a good job on all the actions.

Albre dick was rock hard while he watched Cint suck John's dick. Gage is jacking his dick now, with a blunt in one hand. All of them have gotten head from Cint on those late nights, so Albre don't know why he so excited. Albre said fuck that shit, so he goes to Cint's room and get some condoms. He comes back and put one on. Gage is still stroking his long hard dick, slowly. Albre pulls Cint's dress up and pulls her panties down.

"Wait, wait, what you doing Albre?" Cint pleads.

"Turn around," said Albre motioning for her to turn her ass towards him. John has to turn a little so Cint could still suck his dick while Albre can get the pussy. He noticed that it was kind of tight and dry. After a minute, it gets wet and she was throwing back. He didn't burst because Gage was standing beside him, telling him to let him get some. Therefore, Albre moves and takes the condom off. He starts to masturbate. John gets up, and his dick is hard as a rock in his hand. Albre slides over and let Cint suck his nine-inch dick. John is putting on the last condom off the table. Gage pulls out and goes to the bathroom. So Albre figured he must have reach an organism.

When John starts fucking Cint. She had to stop sucking Albre's dick and starts moaning. Albre was about to cum, so he grabs her head and forced her mouth down on his dick. Albre and John both burst at about the same time. They both go in the bathroom. John flushes the condom and Albre wipes of his dick.

"Man, you crazy," Albre tells John.

"Ole girl pussy was on fire," said John.

"It should be," they both laughed.

John gives Cint a nice piece of crack. Albre leaves her with ten twenties that should last her until in the morning; especially being that the night was slow. John, Gage, and Albre all get in their trucks and head for home.

CHAPTER 10

Albre Drops Bre Off at Janice's House

Albre drops his daughter off at his dad's girlfriend, Janice's house. Janice has been involved with his father for about five years. His mom died when he was ten years old. Janice is the only grandmother his daughter knew on his side.

Janice had known Bre since she was born, and since Shonta and Albre both are going to the Labor Day Bash at Carnes Park. Albre told Shonta that Janice would keep Bre and he would drop her off. Bre was dressed so cute in her Baby Phat outfit and pink and white Air-Maxs as he took her to Janice who was standing on the porch of her Bellwood Estates home.

"Hey Bre, oh you so cute?" Janice said.

"Hi, Grandma Janice," said Bre like a grown woman. Wow! She is growing up so fast, Albre thought.

"Albre, I like your truck. Your dad told me you had painted your truck. It looks nice, but what in the world are you doing with those big rims?" Janice asked.

Janice asked not understanding why youngster these days were so into material things.

"Where are you working?" Janice Albre asked.

Albre knew his dad had told her he wasn't working. At least not an Uncle Sam job.

"Oh, nowhere right now, I'm still in school," said Albre.

"Well, make sure you finish school, and go on to make your dad proud. You know he has worked hard to put you in college. You know he loves you and want you to grow up to be a successful young man," said Janice while motioning for Albre and Bre to follow her in the house.

Janice was living huge. In her half a million-dollar home, in this gated community on the far Eastside of Montgomery. She drove a sixty thousand dollar BMW 745. She was forty-nine years old and worked as an accountant for the city of Montgomery, grossing anywhere to one hundred thousand a year. In addition, she was a member of the all exclusive, BEM, Black Elite Montgomery; and sat on the board of several committees. Nevertheless, her fortune came from the divorce of an ex-husband. He owns an import/export company down in Mobile, Alabama. She divorced her white husband after years of neglecting her for other woman. Janice was a good woman; she had three children, all of them are adults now and have families of their own.

"Well, Janice. I got to go, Shonta's and everybody are probably already at the concert," said Albre.

"See you later, Princess," said Albre to his daughter.

"Bye Daddy!" Bre said.

"Give me a hug before I go," said Albre as he embraces his daughter.

"You gonna make it back in time for the Barbecue or do I need to save you a plate?" Janice tells Albre, as she walks him to the door.

"Just save me a plate, and Bre has a change of clothes in her bag," said Albre.

Out in front of the house where Bre couldn't hear Janice ask Albre for a sack of weed in a low voice. Albre fixes her up a nice quarter ounce of weed, out of his own personal quarter pound.

"You be careful on the road, you know the police are out there everywhere," Janice tells Albre.

Leaving Janice's neighborhood, Albre thinks how one day, he wants to be living in a neighborhood like this particular one or better; a gated community with security, manicured lawns, and no drug activity. A nice place to retire or even raise kids, because Albre was determined to have the better things in life. He's seen a lot and been through a lot. He wanted to accomplish his goal the right way; the legal way. But, he would take it any way it came because he felt like the world owed him that much.

"What's up, John?" Albre speaks into his cell phone.

"Where you at, man?" John asked.

"Oh, I'm on Highway 80, on my way down there no," Albre tells him.

"Well, stop and get some ice. I mean lots of ice and some boxes of Swishers. I sent someone to the store, but hell it's so packed now, it might take them forever to get back," said John.

"Where ya'll gonna be at?" Albre asked.

"When got a tent set up in the front side when you first come in," said John.

"Gage there yet? Shonta around?" Albre asked.

"I see Gage's Suburban from here, and Shonta's with some girl in a convertible Mercedes," said John.

"I'm about 15 minutes away," said Albre.

Albre hangs up the phone, and stop at a Shell Gas Station and get ice and Swishers.

CHAPTER 11

Albre Lost His Pass

"Damn, this bitch is packed," said Albre to himself as he comes up on grid lock about a quarter of a mile from the Park's entrance. Cars were packed all the way back to where he was, beside the road everywhere. But he wasn't about to park his truck. It should take fifteen to thirty minutes to get through traffic and find a place to park.

Albre looked in his rearview mirror and sees a sheriff's car coming up behind him. He steers the big Suburban to the left, so the sheriff cars can get through. When the last sheriff's car came by Albre put the front of his truck out in the road, taking a chance on getting hit by some girls in an Escalade. He cut in front of them and inches forward slowly behind the sheriff's cars. When he's about two hundred yards from the park's entrance. Traffic stopped completely; other deputy sheriffs were directing traffic to a nearby field where everyone had to park and walk the rest of the way. When he got to the deputy sheriff, he motioned for Albre to turn left. Albre tells him he has a VIP pass and he has a ticket.

The sheriff asked, "Where's your pass?" Albre fumbles through his pockets, his glove compartments and couldn't find the pass.

"I can't find it," said Albre frustrated.

"Well move that big ass truck," yells the deputy sheriff. Like on cue, Mike Carnes, Jr. sees Albre and walks over.

"What's the problem, Marco?" Mike asked calling Albre by his real name.

"Man, I got my ticket but I can't find my pass to the Park," said Albre. Albre showed Mike the ticket but he did not have his pass.

Mike was the owner's son so Mike tells the deputy sheriff, "Its okay." He jumps in the passenger side of Albre's Suburban.

"Long time no see," said Mike, "where you been hiding at?"

"I've been going to Alabama State, so I've been low key," said Albre.

"Not from what I heard, and what I see," said Mike referring to Albre's truck.

Mike gets out at the gate where Albre gives the girl at the gate his ticket. He opens his doors and hood so they can do a brief vehicle search.

"I appreciate that, Mike," Albre tells him as he walks off to handle other business.

"See you around," said Mike as he hollers over his shoulder.

"Albre notices everybody checking out his truck while security opens all his doors and check for weapons. He even opens the hood.

"You straight," said the Security.

Albre almost run over people because it was so many walking up. Albre see a big blue tent, on the far front side of the stage. John and Gage's trucks are parked behind it. Gage's back gate to his truck was open. Albre pulls up and park beside Gage's twin Suburban, displaying Luke Freak Feast Cancun on his four TV screens.

When Albre hops out his truck and his Sprewells are still spinning. Albre notices that everybody who is somebody is probably in attendance, showing off their rides, and came to see the Dirty Boyz, and Cash money. The local artist had already performed. Albre looks back at his truck, his Sprewells still spinning, comes to stop.

"Stunt, my nigga, stunt. Your truck is 'stink'," said John while approaching Albre with a Corona in his hand.

"Stink?" Albre asked referring to nice, tight, or cool.

"Man, this motha fucka pack. They didn't want to let me in, but I see Mike. He took care of it," said Albre.

"You got the ice?" John asked.

"Yeah, it's in the trunk," replied Albre.

John had on a blue and navy Rocawear outfit. A Kangol blue fitted cap, and black and dark blue Jordans.

Albre and John walks over to the tent where the rest of the fellows were. Big Boy as on the grill cooking up ribs and steak. All of Albre's friends were sitting around the tent in fold up chairs. There were a couple of women standing around.

"What's up everybody?" Albre speaks to the crew.

"Duke, get the ice out of Albre's truck," John tells Duke.

Duke was John's run around as he was a personal assistance, only he smoke dope and John brought him to run around for him.

"Gage, what's up?" Albre acknowledges his friend.

Albre goes and sits on the cooler beside Gage. Gage was rolling up a blunt, in addition to the several was already rotating around. Gage was dressed fly on his black and white Raider's throw back jersey. Black Polo jeans and black Timberland boots.

"Albre, thought you wasn't coming. Shonta around here somewhere," Gage told him.

"Come on man, you know how I like to make my entrance grand," Albre said as he smiles. Taking the blunt John passes him, he gets up to get himself a cold MGD out of the cooler he was sitting on.

"Say Big Boy, let me get a plate," requests Albre.

He hadn't eaten, so before he started to drink and get fucked up, he needed to put something in his stomach. Albre eats the ribs and potatoes salad, bake beans, and drank an MGC while the Dirty Boys tore the stage up. The crowd went wild, Pimp and Gangsta were performing.

"When them Dirty Boyz drops you better hit the floor. Hit the floor," was coming out the speakers.

John, Gage, and Albre sat around and drinking and smoking while the show goes on. John takes out his camera and goes recording the show. Albre has his camera, but decided to wait until later on to bring his out. John goes to moving about.

"Man, I'm about to go check out some hoes," said John and vanished into the crowd.

Albre goes and get his camera out the truck on his way he sees LaToya with a bunch of her girlfriends, so he goes on to his truck and get his camera.

"What's up?" a female voice said behind him.

"Oh, what's up?" Albre answered in a startled voice.

"Just admiring your truck, oh, whose Suburban is that besides yours?" she asked.

"Yeah, yours look better," she acknowledged.

"Haven't I seen you in Smiley Court?" Albre asked checking her out.

She was looking real scrumptious. Dressed in white and a blue Apple Bottom shirt that fitted real tight around her breasts. You could see her nipples imprint. Her Apple Bottom jeans with a half of apple on her right back pocket, was fitting the same way; tight. Except they were loose around the ankle, and she had on a pair of white and baby blue Air Max.

"Yeah, I'm LaToya. I've seen you out there a lot these last couple of months over at Cint's place," said LaToya.

Albre was surprised that she had taken notice of him.

"Oh, you watch a nigga like that," said Albre while trying to figure out how to work that damn camera recorder.

"Anyway, I'm Albre," he said.

"What are you gonna do with that," LaToya comments.

"You got to make sure the red light is on," said LaToya as she takes the camera and pushes the button.

Of course, Albre didn't know how to work it he had just purchased it about two weeks ago from a crack head named Curt. Once LaToya got it to work, and was satisfied that all the light was working properly, she give it back to Albre.

"Well, well, look who's my first celebrity," said Albre as he zooms in on LaToya. With her pretty honey bun complexion, long dark hair extensions even though she didn't need any.

"Let me take you around here where all my girls at," said LaToya as she leads the way. Albre followed while looking at the screen on his camera which is capturing LaToya's behind.

When they get to the area where LaToya and her friends had set up their tent that was closer to the stage. Albre sees all the gorgeous young women, and of course, where there are ladies, there's niggas. John was already amongst them.

Albre lays his camera down and fire up a blunt of Hydro weed he had in his shirt pocket. Albre look like a million bucks, and he stood out. Which he preferred in a pink, yellow, white, and light brown Enyce outfit, and a pair of beige Bossalino boots. His dreads were almost to his shoulder now, and weren't ragged. They were groomed like most drug dealers, they were real neat because he took the time to get his new growth maintenance every two weeks. LaToya came back with a bottle of Hennessy and a cup of ice.

"Damn, what you trying to do, get me fucked up, early?" Albre asked as he passes LaToya the blunt. She choked and coughed.

"Damn, is that 'Dro?" LaToya asked. Albre confirms and she hit the blunt again and then LaToya walks up beside Albre with his camera.

"What you on?" John asked referring to Albre's drink.

"Hen dog," Albre replies as he gives John the bottle off the table.

"Damn, is that the mystical LaToya? Hell, she looks real sweet to me. No way is she a gold digger. She's too young to have any game," said John. John was flipping his brand new Sony camera on and Albre smiles.

"Say Albre, she's calling you to come join her," said John not knowing Albre had every intention of joining her in more ways than one.

Albre allows his camera to hang down around his neck while he pimp walks over with his Hennessey in one hand and a blunt in the other. They don't talk. Albre just stands there while LaToya dances and is throwing that ass all sexually up on him. Albre thinks, damn this is what it feels like to have money and fame.

CHAPTER 12

Carnes Park

In the meantime at Carnes Park, Powell and Scooby are sitting in a candy red with tan vinyl interior Crown Victoria that is sitting on some 20" Spiders. The Crown Victoria also has black tinted windows, and a dent on the passenger side door where someone had backed into Scooby's car. They had been parked on the left side of the stage since they came. They were in the car sniffing cocaine when Powell noticesAlbre.

"Ain't that's one of those city niggas?" Powell asked Scooby.

"Where at?" Scooby asked with powder on his nose. Before Powell can answer, Scooby goes, "I see him, that's Albre," said Scooby.

"Where's that dude John at? I saw his truck earlier," said Powell

Powell and Scooby are known for putting the pistol down on drug dealers. They had heard Albre was making a lot of money in Smiley Court. They had robbed John some years back and got away with it. John was clueless to who had robbed him or so they thought. Gage being his usual self had been drinking all day and was sitting in his truck with this girl he had met name Zelinka.

By the time, Albre and John got back to their tent. The concert was almost over and Cint and Big Boy were packing everything up.

"Albre I put the cooler in your truck with the rest of the beer and liquor in it," said Cint. She had ridden down with Big Boy in his Ford F-150.

"You know it's after party at Club Platinum back in the city," John tells Albre.

"Hell yeah, I plan on going, the night hasn't even began yet. Shit, you can ride with me," Albre tells John.

When the concert was over, and since they were parked in the park, not side the Highway. They had a difficult time getting out. It was so crowded with cars and people. Albre was behind John's Expedition. Gage was behind Albre in his Suburban. Cars had stopped moving and Albre was getting frustrated when LaToya walked up to the driver side window.

"Hey, you. You coming out to Club Platinum tonight?" LaToya asked.

"Yeah. I'll be there," said Albre.

"Well, I'll see you tonight," said LaToya as she sashayed off.

When cars start to move again. Albre sees Shonta sitting behind the wheel of a gray Mercedes convertible.

"Hey, Shonta," Albre gets her attention.

"Hey, what's up? Shonta spoke back.

She was looking good; her hair was done, face made up, and her pearly white teeth beautifully gleaning with a diamond's sparkle.

"I'm bringing Bre home in the morning," Albre tells his baby momma.

"Okay," said Shonta.

"Hey, hold up," said Albre.

He stopped his truck, Shonta gets out the Mercedes and runs up to the passenger side window.

"Can I please borrow some money?" Shonta begs.

"Damn, Shonta. Did you get the job at the hospital?" Albre asked. It was unpleasant that Shonta was asking for money like this.

"Yeah, I just started, dummy. I haven't gotten paid, yet," said Shonta.

Albre pulls out his knot of money; he peels off five 100-dollar bills, and gives it to Shonta.

"Have a good time, Shonta," Albre tells her.

"Thank you, Al," said Shonta.

He hated when Shonta called him Al instead of Albre. But he smiles, he loved his baby momma. They just couldn't see eye to eye.

When Albre gets back to the city, he goes to Cint's apartment. Gage was there already. Cint was in her bedroom-smoking crack as he walks in; Cint comes out the back bedroom looking geeked up.

`   "Albre let me get some dope?" Cint asked.

Albre thinks to himself, that he's tired of this shit already and this life ain't for him. He goes into the other bedroom, which he and Gage only has keys.

"Here, Cint," said Albre as he gives her a hundred dollar piece because she did hold it down at the tent today.

"Hello," John answers the phone, sounding out of breath.

"I'm on my way," Albre tells him. They leave out of Smiley Court, headed to pick John up in Westwood.

"Oh, alright, that's what's up!" John said and hung up the phone.

Albre slows down on his way to John's house. John stayed behind Edgewood in the newer section of Westwood Estates, where it was safe to leave your car parked on the street. Albre spotted a city police car coming up behind him and he gets nervous because he has this pistol on him, and weed and ain't no telling what the fuck Gage had on him. He wasn't in the mood to take the police on a high-speed chase until he could throw everything. Luckily, the police car turned off on another street and Albre was able to breathe easy. When he pulled up to John's street, he can see John sitting on the hood of his Impala in the dark. He could see the light from his phone clearly.

When they reached Club Platinum, it was packed, and Albre couldn't find a place to park so he double-parked to the left of the door to the club, behind a Ford Mustang. When the threesome approached the door, they didn't have to wait in line. They were recognized immediately by one of the bouncers Big Rick has at the club. The bouncer's name was Junior. Junior was an ex-wrestler, professional. They all paid their own way in, and because John knows Big Rick, and has spent thousands of dollars at his club, Big Rick meets them at the door and escorts them to the VIP section.

"On me John," said Big Rick as he opens the door. He lets them in VIP for free. He knew they were gonna spend some money.

"Yeah, you know we came to spend some money, you slick ole bastard," John complains with a smirk on his face.

"You always been a baller, VIP material. Don't stop now," said Big Rick.

They all go in and sit on the plush sofa, and chairs in the VIP section where numerous celebrities have sat in the same chairs.

"Man, this room is a hoe magnet. Luke himself blessed this room," Big rick tells him as he signals for the waitress.

"What can I get for you guys?" the big-breasted waitress asked.

"A case of Coronas, a setup of Remy Martin VSOP, and three bottles of Moet at least six years old," said John giving orders like the veteran, he was.

"And a setup every thirty minutes, something," Albre comments as the waitress leaves. Because they came to have a great time.

And with the threesome, there was no telling what might happen, the sky's the limit.

"Let me be on the move," said Big Rick.

"We getting kind of pack, I'm gonna have to tell the door to stop letting people in."

"You wouldn't turn down no money, Big Rick. You don't care if you violate every code, the Montgomery fire and safety commission set," John jokes.

"Ain't that the truth, man," said Big Rick as he laughs all hearty and leaves.

Before the waitress could come back with the Cognac and Champagne, the V.I.P. section was getting packed, wall to wall with women. Some of them Albre knew and some he didn't, but he brought drinks for them all. It has more action in that room than on the dance floor. Gage left to go to the truck. He came back with some cocaine, and started laying it out on a tray on the table. Albre laced a blunt with the cocaine as John and Gage sniffed powder and passed it around to all the people that they didn't know. Before Albre knew it, they were getting served back to back setups of Remy Martin and Moet. He and John was tossing money left and right. The Moet alone cost a hundred dollars a bottle, and he could see at least twelve amongst them. Albre was tipsy, but wasn't drunk yet. He stood and looked out at the dance floor. There she was, LaToya, standing alone and she was beautiful. She looked up at Albre, and they just stared at each other as if they were the only ones in the club. Albre leaves the V.I.P. section and heads for the direction he saw LaToya.

"Albre," someone calls him from behind. He turns and sees Nikki standing in his shadow.

"What's up, Nikki? Albre asked.

"Oh, I haven't seen you in a while. You stop returning my calls. I thought maybe I wouldn't run into you ever again," said Nikki.

"Well, yeah, I've been busy these last couple of months," said Albre.

They just stood there looking at each other. Albre starts to feel uncomfortable and he needed to find LaToya.

"I guess I'll see you later," said Albre.

He continued to push through the crowd in the direction he last seen LaToya. He spots her leaning over on the DJ's booth. She notices him as he walks over.

CHAPTER 13

Albre Meets LaToya

"Hey, sexy. You must be from Tennessee?" Albre asked LaToya.

She decided to play along with him.

"No, why?" LaToya asked.

"Because you're the only Ten-I-See," Albre replies.

"You're really crazy," said LaToya as she gets out between laughter.

"Hey, can I get this dance? Before I get too drunk and you have to pick me up off the floor," said Albre.

"Sure, I don't think you would ever allow that to happen to you," said LaToya as she led Albre to the floor.

As if by request, the DJ plays Usher's *"Nice and Slow"*. Albre sings along with Usher while looking into LaToya's eyes. God, she's fine, he thinks while his hand gently moves down to her butt, exploring the curves of her body. While moving over the soft fabric of her Baby Phat outfit. LaToya is shorter than Albre and he's 5'9". She looks up and blinks her eyes at Albre all seductively, and Albre knew right then that he had to have this girl. They danced to about four more songs and LaToya had him so hard and hot. He wanted to make love to her, right there on the floor.

"What are you doing after the club?" Albre asked.

"I'm going to get something to eat, and go home. Isn't that what young ladies do?" LaToya said while putting a lot of emphasis on "ladies."

"Yeah, I guess you're too young to hang out with the lions and tigers, and bears," said Albre.

"You can say I'm afraid of what goes on with the lions, tigers, and bears, especially when they drink," said LaToya.

"Well, you right about that. You shouldn't be out here in the wee hours of the night. I've seen little girls taken advantage of too many times," said Albre.

"I'm not a little girl and I can handle myself. But I'm the D.D.," said LaToya explaining her early departure.

"What's a D.D.?" Albre asked.

"Designated driver," answers LaToya matter of factly.

Albre sees John talking loud over by the bar and Gage seemed to be chain smoking.

"Yeah, I'm glad I ain't have too much drink. It looks like I'm the Designated Driver also," said Albre.

As him and LaToya exchange numbers for the second time in twenty-four hours, they both go their separate ways to perform their duties as their friend's caretaker for the night. Albre gathered up John and Gage and when they reached John's house it was 4 a.m. He dropped off John, and then Gage. When he finally gets home, his cell phone rings.

"Hello," said Albre as he lights a Black & Mild with his Bic disposable lighter.

"Just checking to make sure you made it home safe," said LaToya.

"I just pulled up in the yard. How did things go with you?" Albre asked.

"Well, I decided Toni and Adrian could stay at my house, so they're already asleep. Toni threw up in the rental. Oh, she'll clean it out before I return it Monday. At least somebody will. I'm not cleaning it up," said

LaToya.

"Can I call you in the morning?" Albre asked.

"Yeah," said LaToya.

That was all Albre remembered of that night. He doesn't even remember making it into the house, leaving his keys in the front door and crashing on his bed.

CHAPTER 14

Albre Has More than Enough Dope

Albre is exhausted from going to school every day and selling dope in Smiley Court into the late hours. As he, leaves school his cell phone rings.

"Hello!" Albre answers.

"Yo, Albre this John. I need you to meet meat the safe house in King Hill in twenty minutes, so we can go holla at Cash," John tells him.

"I'm leaving school now, I'll be out there in a few," said Albre.

"Check. When you see my car park in front of the house," said John, "call me when you outside."

"Alright," said Albre.

He ended the call and heads the back way to King Hill because traffic was heavy at four o'clock in the afternoon. Albre turned on to King Hill Street. He knows John sells dope out here. But he doesn't like his car to be seen out here. He was already being investigated by the police. Therefore, he knew they knew his car. He pulls behind John's '69 Impala and calls him on the phone. Before coming out of the house.

"What's up?" John said as he was getting in Albre's car.

"You know, school's wearing me down," said Albre.

"Nah, them streets wearing you down, Pimp," said John.

Albre drives off heading in the direction of his house in Ridgecrest.

"We got to be at Cash Jewelry Store in thirty minutes," John tells him.

"I got to go by the house to get this money," explained Albre.

Albre reaches his house in Ridgecrest in fifteen minutes. He goes in and come back out with his pack. When he gets in the car, John is counting his money.

Albre and John heads to Top Knotch Jewelry to buy some dope from Cash, who owns the jewelry store. He has been to Top Knotch on different occasions to buy jewelry, but never to purchase drugs.

"I'm gonna introduce you to Cash," said John, "he already knows about you."

"I got cha," replied Albre.

Cash's office was located on Fairview Avenue. Albre drives in that direction. When they get to Top Knotch Jewelry, Albre leaves his backpack and grab the money. When they enter the store. They were met by a black girl, wearing a nametag that introduces her as Jazz.

"Cash, you got a guy out here who say he come to pick up his Rolex," Jazz quietly talks into the phone.

"Let them come back here," said Cash .

Jazz let them through the counter and escorted them to the back where Cash's office was located. Then she returned to the front of the store because there was one customer looking at the cases of jewelry.

John knocked on the door of Cash's office and Cash opened the door, and let them into the office. Albre checks out the scene. He notices how the office was setup. Cash has a big mahogany desk with a computer to the right on another smaller desk. There was a picture of Nigeria behind the desk that Cash had sat in and no window but a couple of file cabinets and a standing safe to the left of where Cash standing at his desk. But he knew that Cash more than likely to have about five safes in this store.

"Have a seat, gentlemen," said Cash as he motioned to the chair in front of his desk.

"John, I assume that this is Albre?" Cash asked.

"Oh yeah, this is my partner Albre," said John, "he be out in Smiley Court."

"What can I do for you guys?" Cash said as he looked at Albre.

"I want to do business with you if your price is right," Albre tells Cash.

"It depends on what and how much as you can see I probably have what you want," said Cash.

He motions his hands across his store as if he was talking about jewelry. But Albre knows he's talking about drugs.

"I want 5 ounces, soft," Albre tells him referring to cocaine as soft in its powder form.

"I tell you what, check this out," said Cash.

He produces a Ziploc bag of cocaine from behind his desk and places it on the desk.

"Taste it," he tells Albre.

Albre picks up the cocaine and sticks his finger in there and took the cocaine on his finer and places it on his tongue. His tongue became really numb instantly .

"Damn, that's the shit," said Albre while placing the bag back on the table.

"And there's plenty more where that came from, tell him John," said Cash through laughter.

Laughing at the expression on Albre's face.

"Yeah, Cash can get you anything you want, Albre," said John, "I mean the best of the best. I don't know who he knows, but I sho would like to know."

"I bet you would," said Cash as he smiled at them, "now, I'll let you get five ounces for six hundred a piece. But since you came with John, I'll let you have it for $450."

Albre was nervous and breathless. This was the connection he was looking for with cocaine this raw and for this price, he was sure to come up quick.

"Hell, for that price, let me get seven ounces," said Albre. He had brought three grand with him. Since he was getting it for so low, he added the extra one fifty out of his spending money.

"Look, bottom line is John tells me you have Smiley Court on lock with the crack. So I'm gonna help you lock down the whole Southside," said Cash.

"Man, with this hook up you giving me, I'm sure you would love my business," said Albre

"Well, here's seven ounces," said Cash as he pulls out more cocaine and weighs it on the jewelry triple beam scale, until he is satisfied with the quantity.

"Here's my pager number Albre. Call me and leave your number, and I'll call you back in ten minutes," explains Cash, "if I don't call back then I'm not able to be reached, understand?"

"Yeah, I got you. Here's my cell phone number, so you will know when I page you," said Albre, "and nice doing business with you."

"Later, man," said Cash.

"Albre, wait for me out front, let me holler at Cash," John tells him.

He goes back to the front of the store with dope locked around his waist.

"You have what I wanted?" John asked Cash.

"Yeah," said Cash as he pulls out a brown grocery paper bag.

John examines the weed inside. He wanted 20 pounds of weed. He could tell that it looked right, even though it was compressed. He gives Cash the money and grabs the brown paper bag. Cash doesn't count the money and John doesn't weight the weed. They had been doing business since Rico got popped, and had established some level of trust.

"Hey, here's an ounce of crack," said Cash as he gives John another package, "for turning me on to Albre."

John takes the ounce and puts it in the waist of his pants. They shake hands and John walks back out to the front of the store. Albre knows John is getting a cut from Cash for bringing him business, that's why he was excused from the office. When John walks out the front with the paper bag, he sees Albre examining the cases of jewelry.

"See something you want?" John asked.

"Not today, just window shopping," said Albre as he looked at the Rolex, Marc Jacobs, and Seiko watches, knowing soon he would probably own all of them and at great length.

"Thanks for introducing me to Cash," Albre tells John as they are sitting in John's car.

"Yeah, he's cool. He must like you or either he thinks you are going to make him a lot of money, because I never seen him drop his prices like that," said John.

"Yeah, I was surprised at how cheap he let me get the dope," said

Albre.

"So be careful, fucking with Cash. He looks like Kemmit the Frog, but he is a maliciously dangerous man, and he has the right connections," said John, "so be all business with him, because he most definitely has his plans for you and all that talk about taking over the Southside."

"I know, man, he must not know that is impossible," said Albre.

"Well, it's not impossible, but I doubt if Slim OG would allow you to take over," said John.

The mention of Slim OG, the leader of the Bloodz on the Southside who was supplying most of the Southside from Englewood to Cedar Park.

"Hell, and the Roc. Man I ain't trying to step on them guys' toes," said Albre.

Albre was thinking about the retaliation from Slim OG and Roc if he was to start suddenly supplying the Southside.

"Sometimes to get to the top, you have to step on some people," said John.

"I know but you talking about stepping on Slim OG and Roc," said Albre.

"Damn, Albre. I thought you wanted to get money. I know you not showing fear. You just gotta move your location and start setting up shops in different areas. Expansion my guy, expansion," John tells him, looking at Albre while he drives searching for a facial expression. He didn't see any because Albre was in deep thought, "see, you move locations. Setup different shops all over the Southside and open shop at all location at the same time. You got them young niggas in Smiley that looks up to you and wants to make some money."

"Yeah, I could put somebody in each location. Hell with Cash backing me. I should have more than enough dope," said Albre, "I'll think about it."

Albre drops John off in King Hill and goes to his trap in Smiley Court.

CHAPTER 15

Albre Sees LaToya

"You coming to pick me up or what?" LaToya asked Albre.

"Yes, what time will you be ready?" Albre asked.

"Kim should be done with my hair in a minute. Pick me up at 6 o'clock," LaToya tells him.

He said he would and then they hung up the phone. Albre had been seeing a lot of LaToya lately. Going places with her, taking her to the movies, to the park, and to the mall. He even took her out to dinner at Omar's where they both had to dress formal. Albre enjoyed evenings out with LaToya. She was very respectable, has great table manners, and didn't order the most expensive meal on the menu.

Albre was in Smiley Court, at the trap and Cint was gone in his car. Hell, he had to pick LaToya up in 30 minutes and he was cursing Cint out, wishing she would come back in his car. Cint finally pulls up.

"Damn, bitch. Where you been? To Atlanta or somewhere?" Albre barks at Cint as she gets out the car.

"Man, you ask me to drop off dope at the traps. I wasn't trying to speed with more than a brick in the car," said Cint.

Albre knew she was right. She did have to distribute a brick, between three different locations. Albre had decided to expand over the Westside after talking it over with John and Gage. Now, he had four traps and been in business about three weeks. He was already feeling the heat from Roc. But none of Slim OG's gang came around yet. Albre knew it was just a matter of time.

Albre continued to sell dope out of Cint's apartment in Smiley Court. Gage was slanging out the trap over in Brickdale and Conan was over Southlawn, Ali was at the Peddler Inn.

All four traps were moving more than a brick a week. Albre was now getting six to eight brick (kilos) at a time from Cash and he was paying seventeen five a brick. Everybody was making money and Albre had saved one hundred and ninety thousand since he started selling dope in June.

Albre arrives at Unique Styles Salon and LaToya was waiting outside.

"Hey," said Albre as she gets in the car.

"Hey, Albre," said LaToya as she leans over and kisses him.

"I like your braids," said Albre.

He comments LaToya's hair. She had micro braids that were so small; it had to be a thousand braids, and Albre knows that she probably paid about two hundred dollars for the hairstyle.

"What you about to do, Albre?" LaToya asked.

"I got to go back to the trap. Why?" Albre asked

"Can I use your car to go to the mall?" LaToya asked him.

"Yeah, just drop me off at Cint's apartment. You need some money?" Albre asked.

"Naw, I still got the money you gave me yesterday," said LaToya.

LaToya was a senior in George Washington Carver High and she was an A student, working on an Advanced Diploma, so Albre didn't really want her to work, but focus on her school.

LaToya drops him off at Cint's apartment and heads off to the mall.

When Albre walks in the apartment, Cint is cooking which was good because Albre was hungry. It smelled like she was cooking fried chicken and rice.

"Damn, Cint, something smells good," said Albre.

"Just cooking some chicken. I figure you must be hungry," said Cint.

"Starved," said Albre

"It'll be done in a minute," said Cint.

Traffic started to pick up and Albre couldn't even enjoy his food, having to make a sell every time he sat down.

Albre finally finished his food and sits on the front porch. It's getting dark outside. But, Albre notices this beat up Van. It has been sitting there all day. He just noticed it had been sitting there a couple of days ago. But it was parked farther down the block. Now, it's parked closer to Luther Street, the street Cint's apartment is on.

"Hey, Cint," Albre calls for Cint.

"What's up?" Cint asked.

"You noticed that green van lately?" Albre asked.

"That beat up one?" Cint asked.

"Yeah," said Albre.

"Oh, I see it. It was parked around the corner on Fry Street yesterday," said Cint.

"Have someone check it out for me," said Albre.

He walks back in the apartment because if it was the Narcos, he didn't want them to know that he knew that they were watching him.

Cint goes out the back door of the apartment to check on the van from across the street. Albre sells dope all night. Cint had told him it didn't appear to be any activity in the van. When LaToya brought the car back after shopping, Albre took her home to her mom's apartment around the block. When he got back, the van was gone.

Albre sat down on the sofa, thinking of the events of the last months. He hadn't been with LaToya sexually, but he knew he was falling in love because she dominated his thoughts and he wants to be in her company all the time. However, these last couple of weeks, especially he hasn't had time for no girls or much of anything with school and trying to run an organization.

Albre's glad he's in his last year at Alabama State. In May, he would receive his BA in Business and Market Management, and his MA in Political Science. And he would be glad when May came, because he was getting tired of the street life already.

CHAPTER 16

King Hill Street

"Hello," Albre answered.

"Albre, where you at?" Gage said sounding hysterical and breathing into the phone nervously.

Gage called him on his cell phone at school. Something had to be wrong. No one called him on his cell while he was at school. They always paged him.

"Man, I'm at school. What's up?" Albre said sensing something wrong.

"Man, they just robbed the safehouse in Southlawn," said Gage.

"Who? Was anybody hurt?" Albre asked.

"Nah, man. But they shot the place up. Police out here everywhere," said Gage.

"Where's Conan?" Albre asked.

"He's on his way out here to Brickdale. He left the girl that rented the apartment there to talk to the police," said Gage.

"Hey, you and Conan meet me at John's safehouse in King Hill and call Ali and tell him to be there now," said Albre and then he hung up the phone.

When his phone rang, he had removed himself from his History class. So he sticks his head in the door and tells Professor Wright that it was an emergency and asked him if he could be excused from class. Professor Wright gave him the okay. So now, he was high tailing it over to King

Hill. King Hill was where John had one of his traps and it was closer to Alabama State. So Albre didn't want to be seen meeting at one of his traps that's why he told them to meet him in King Hill.

"John, where you at?" Albre asked.

"I'm in King Hill. What's up?" John asked.

"I'm on my way over there, Conan just got robbed in Southlawn; and I told everyone to meet me over there," said Albre.

"That's cool," said John. "I'll clear everybody out by the time you get here."

"Aight," said Albre.

He ends the call and turns on King Hill Street five minutes later. Ten minutes after that he arrived and Gage pulls up in his Suburban with Conan. Then Ali pulls up in his Mustang, while Gage and Conan was coming in. The room was dark, the curtain was drawn and the only light came from a standing lamp over in the corner. John, Albre, Gage, Conan, Ali were all sitting at the table as if they were about to play some poker. The air was stale and you could tell it was a drug house by the stuff laying around on the floor. Tobacco that came out of opened cigars for rolling blunts and disposable lighters along with all sorts of trash. The tension around the table was building; no one said a word. They were waiting for their time to talk. The trap in Southlawn was the one brining in the most money and Conan was handling more than a brick a day by himself.

"First, what did you tell him to tell the police when you left her at the house?" Albre asked and you could hear his voice echoing.

"I told her to only tell them that it was a drive by. Not to mention anything about a robbery, especially nothing to do with drugs," said

Conan calmly.

"Good. Now what did they take?" Albre asked..

"Damn, Albre. I didn't see them coming. They just pulled up and jumped out with red flags wrapped around their faces. I didn't have time to pull out my piece," Conan said as he catches his breath between smokes of his Black & Milds and then continues, "they were in two cars, a gray Crown Victoria 93' and a 93' Lincoln Town Car. They made away with 7 ounces of crack, 12 ounces of soft, about 3 pounds of Hydro, and 79 hundred dollars." As he finished talking, and then looks at Albre.

Albre's not surprised because he knew Conan handled that type of weight. But the weed was probably his own, and he probably got it from John. Albre always had Cint cook up the dope before distributing it.

"What you just had the dope lying around?" Albre asked.

"Nah, I was weighing and sacking the dope up," said Conan.

"I'm glad nobody got hurt," said Albre, "fuck the dope. It can be replaced."

"So you're pretty sure it was Slim OB's gang?" John asked.

"Yeah, it had to be. All those red bandannas," replied Conan.

"So this is what we gonna do because this is such a bug, an unexpected loss. Since we know that the police are probably gonna be watching, we gonna change operations. Conan you will be handling the weight for John on the weed tip out of the house on Southlawn. Give it two weeks and then crank it up with the weed," said Albre and looks at John for approval. John nods his head in a yes of approval.

"Ali, we gonna have to put somebody with you at the inn because we are going to double your supply, since you are the closest to Southlawn.

Conan can send all the crack and cocaine business your way and you send all the week business his way," said Albre and then continues, "who do you want at the inn with you, Ali?"

"I'll have Ricky come down and chill with me," said Ali. That was cool with Albre and John because Ricky was John's cousin.

"Albre, Cint tells me they are watching you out there in Smiley Court," said Gage.

He finally spoke; everyone looks at Gage and then back to Albre. "Yeah, it's this green beat up van that's been parked out there watching me. That's why I'm about to triple operation in Smiley Court to draw all the attention to me. Then I'm gonna lose shop, so please stay away from me because the police is probably watching me and stay away from Smiley Court," said Albre.

"Gage spot in Brickdale is not under surveillance or anything, right?" John asked.

"Nah, I've been moving some weight. But it's pretty slow right now," said Gage.

"Any way, we knew we was gonna draw heat from Slim OB. Have anyone seen any of Roc's guys around?" John asked.

Everyone said no, but Albre didn't like that not one bit.

"So we are not gonna retaliate on Slim OB right now. We'll wait until I say the time is right," said Albre.

Albre already knew that they would wait until after Christmas because Slim OB wouldn't strike again before then. They would know Albre knew it's them. They would be waiting for Albre to retaliate but would be surprised when it didn't happen.

"Look, if this happens again, it ain't worth your life my niggas. Give them what they want," said Albre.

"I know that's right," agrees John.

Everyone departed King Hill Street thinking about their new duties. But Albre departed thinking about if only he could make it until graduation and he would leave this lifestyle to Gage, John, Conan, and Ali.

CHAPTER 17

Everything was Going According to Plan

Everything was going according to plan. Albre was making more money in Smiley Court than the rest of the traps combined. They haven't heard anything else from Slim OB's gang or the Roc and everyone was making money. Cash was gone on vacation in the Caribbeans for Christmas and left Albre a U-storage-It garage filled with dope. But it was way out in the country – a place on the outside of Selma called Plantersville, Alabama.

Albre and LaToya were spending more time together. Albre had finally made love to LaToya one night when she came over to Cint's apartment while they were the only ones there. Albre remember that night at the end of November vividly. They have been inseparable since.

"Daddy, can I have a cotton candy?" Bre said looking at Albre questionably.

He and LaToya were Christmas shopping. LaToya wanted to buy everything Bre wanted of course. She just adored Bre, and that made her even that more irresistible to Albre.

"Sure, what color, Chipmunk?" Albre asked Bre playfully.

"Pink, and I'm not a chipmunk. I am a princess," said Bre.

"Yes, you are a princess, Chipmunk," said Albre, and they started laughing.

Christmas was in two more weeks and Albre's baby momma, Shonta, was putting in many hours at the hospital. So Albre was always keeping

Desperate Days - Bo Hall

Bre, or else she was at his grandmother's house.

They left the mall in Albre's Suburban. LaToya was driving the Cutlass to school every day so Albre let her keep it at her apartment. Albre drops Bre off at his grandmother's house and he and LaToya heads to the movies to see a new release. Albre stops at a gas station on his way to Winsor Cinemas. He purchases a Swiser blunt and fills his truck up with gas. As he gets the gas and he sees this white Lexus pull up. He recognized the occupants as Powell and Scooby. Two country niggas that like to rob. Word was that they were the ones who had robbed John a couple of years ago. However, they seem to have disappeared. By them resurfacing again, that couldn't be good. They just watched Albre before the driver Powell decided to get out. Albre finished pumping his gas and got in the driver side of his truck where LaToya was waiting. Albre rolls his blunt with the Swiser he had just bought. While watching Powell and Scooby watch him.

"Who are those guys?" LaToya asked following Albre eyes to the two black guys in the white Lexus.

"Oh, they ain't no body," said Albre.

He throws the truck in drive and continues to the movies while smoking his blunt. When they reached the movies, both he and LaToya were high. Winsor Cinema wasn't that busy for a Friday night. But they had three screens showing the movie, the new release because it was so highly anticipated, all three theaters were packed. Albre and LaToya made their way to the back where they could see the movie and everything else going on. Because it was so dark in movies that would be dangerous.

The movie lasted two hours and LaToya and Albre laugh so hard,

LaToya started crying once. They were high, so everything was funny to them.

After the movies, Albre took LaToya to a nice five-star hotel down town. They checked into a suite at the Marriott. The suite they checked into was extravagant and expensive. The bathroom quarters had standing showers, his and hers sinks, and a hot tub. The living quarter had antique furniture décor and a full bar. The bedroom had a King size bed and a balcony that looked out upon the Riverfront over the Alabama River; the view was breath taking. Albre ordered a bottle of Dom Perignon Champagne. As they waited on the champagne, LaToya ran water in the Jacuzzi. When the champagne finally did arrived, Albre brought the champagne and two glasses into the bathroom where LaToya was already in the Jacuzzi. All he could see was bubbles, and he couldn't sit the bottle and glass down and get out of his robe fast enough to explore what was under those bubbles. He slides in the Jacuzzi, hands LaToya her glass then pours them a generous amount of Dom Perighon. He moved closer to LaToya, bubbles over flowing the tub. When their bodies meet, his hands roamed over her body pulling her close to him. He kissed her, and she kissed him back. Their kisses are deep and their breaths are shallow. Albre kisses her neck and gently lifts her out the water. He blows the soap off her nipples and indulges it in his mouth. She offers him the other breast because the other nipple was getting jealous.

Soon they find themselves on the white satin sheets of the king-size bed. The balcony door is open so the river breeze of the night air rushes in. LaToya lies on her back while Albre takes to all parts of her body with his mouth. She moans, and wiggles to pull free from him. But his grip is strong, he pulls her back to him. She arches her back as he kisses her side. He makes his way down to the inside of her thigh and forces her to open her legs. He kisses her passionately, but roughly. He kisses the other inner thigh.

LaToya moans, "Stop, oh please, stop."

He doesn't hear her as he takes her to his mouth. She moans more and grabs his head. He uses his tongue and his lips to play with her most precious jewel.

"Oh, Albre, ba ba baby," she screams in a high pitch as she reaches ecstasy.

Albre mounts her, kissing her over so gently on her lips. She's still shaking and Albre puts his throbbing rod inside her. She's so moist, and the feeling is unbelievable. He grinds in a slow motion at first.

"LaToya, oh baby, its good. It's so good baby," he cries tears of pleasure.

Then he stops and turns her over on her belly, and tells her to get on her knees and hand. She does as she's told. He stands up over the bed, and pulls her back to him so that her ass is arched up and all of her wet pussy is exposed. He stands on his tip toes and slide back inside her. They fit as if they are a perfect match. He's quickly in and out of her in that motion. Pulling her to him with great force and then with not so great force; and when he gets ready to cum they both cried out, "Oh…" and they exploded in unison.

Then they fall asleep from exhaustion. Albre woke up to find LaToya taking him into her mouth. Her hand gently strokes his hard wood and she looks up at him with those soft eyes with her mouth full of him. He's tense and relaxed as she crawls up and straddles him. She rides him. He grabs both her breast and pulls her to him. She pushes him back down and continues to ride him in a motion that he cums in minutes. She looks down at him with satisfaction. No words were exchanged. He was in love beyond comparison. She felt as if she had just conquered him and that she had him for sure.

CHAPTER 18

A Week before Christmas

A week before Christmas, Albre sits in his newly purchased apartment in Vaughn Heights. His two-bedroom apartment overlooks a lake in a gated community of an upper class neighborhood. He has only had this apartment for a week. His only furniture is his bed that he took from his dad house. His other furniture hasn't been delivered, yet.

Albre sits on the floor and counts the money he has made these last couple of weeks. He already has 190 thousand dollars stored in a safe deposit box in Atlanta under an alias name. He has closed down his trap in Smiley court a day before he purchases this apartment only three people knows of this apartment. When he finishes counting his money, he has a total of 275 thousand. He puts this money in a duffle bag and heads out to his dad Lincoln Navigator that he had borrowed. Albre takes this money to Atlanta, which is three hours' drive. He puts the money in the safe deposit box along with the money already there.

Since Albre closed down the trap in Smiley Court, Cint has moved to another part on the backside of Smiley Court. But she is always at the trap in Brickdale where Gage sells dope at.

When Albre comes back from Atlanta, he goes to Peddler inn, where Ali and Rick are at. Ali and Rick have been holding down this trap and have been moving a lot of dope. So much traffic has been coming through. They have started to draw attention from the drug task force. Albre has already been paying extra money to the owner of the hotel, so he can keep his mouth shut.

"What's up, Albre?" Ali asked as lab gets out the car.

Albre has it setup so that Ali and Rick have adjoining room where they keep the dope in one room and sell out the other. But they are constantly changing room.

"I'm aight. What's the move?" Albre said noticing Rick in the window looking out.

"You now busy as usual," said Ali.

"Well, you can expect a lot more traffic, since I close the shop down in Smiley Court," said Albre.

"Yeah, we already getting the business," said Ali.

"Well, leave Rick here and come with me to Brickdale," said Albre.

"Aight, let me go put this up," said Ali.

While going back in the hotel room to put the dope up. When he comes back he and Albre go to Southlawn to pick up Conan and they all ride together to Brickdale, where Gage and Cint are at. When they arrive, Gage Suburban is parked out front. They all get out and go in.

"What's up, Gage?" Albre said and they all exchanged greetings.

"Man, I tried to call you early today. I had someone wanted to buy three bricks," Gage tells Albre.

"Well, I was handling some business," said Albre, "you can call him back and arrange an exchange."

"Check. It's not a him, it's a her," Gage smiles.

"Whatever, call her back tell her it's on," said Albre.

They were all seated in the living room. Cint was in the bedroom, probably smoking dope.

"Look, Roc sent somebody at me to tell me that we are knocking his business, and I can either cut him on the money, or I close down shop on the Southside; also he wants twenty percent..." he paused to make sure everyone was listening, "what do ya'll think?"

Gage was the first one to speak, "Well, I say we cut him in, but only ten percent. Because we don't need the heat from him; we already got Slim OG to worry about."

"Fuck him," said Conan. Which was to be expected from him since he was the hardheaded type.

"Yeah, I say we just pop a cap in his ass, and drop him in the river," said Ali.

"It ain't that simple. Even if we do that, he got people who would want revenge," said Albre as he tries to calm the two young niggas down and then continues, "look, I say we cut him in the twenty percent, just until after the New Year. By then we will have been taken care of Slim OG. Because Slim OG is our main threat right now."

"Well, it might work. But only until after New Year," said Gage.

"I don't know; he might be up to something. It might be a trick," said Ali.

"Well, I don't think he'll turn down the twenty percent, and it's only until after New Year," said Albre, "and we will find a way to get the Roc off our backs."

"Aight. I'm with it," said Gage.

"Me, too," said Ali.

"I guess I'm outnumbered," said Conan not liking giving the Roc twenty percent. Because they are the ones taking penitentiary chances.

After they all agreed, they stayed an extra hour and plotted on how to take Slim OG out on New Year's Eve.

CHAPTER 19

On Christmas Day

On Christmas, everybody was enjoying themselves. Albre was at his baby momma, Shonta's apartment when Bre woke up on Christmas day. Bre was so happy with her many gifts, but she was ecstatic when she opened her gift from Santa Claus and saw it was a pink Barbie Jeep that she wanted so much. Albre and Shonta had bought each other gifts. Shonta bought him a set of Armani cologne and a 14-karat gold money clip. Albre brought her a pink diamond ankle bracelet and gave her a bank draft for a ten thousand dollars account in her name at Region Bank. Shonta was grateful to have a baby daddy like Albre.

Later that day everyone gather at Albre father's house. His uncle Kevin, his dad's twin brother was there. Cint and her sister, Janice, who is his dad's girlfriend was there. Along with a host of cousins, aunts, and uncles. Albre brought LaToya along with him, Gage, Ali, Conan was all there and everyone was having a good time sitting around eating, drinking, and smoking. His dad didn't allow them to smoke weed in front of the house, so Albre, Gage, Ali, and Conan sneaks out back while everyone was occupied in deep conversation and the spirit of Christmas.

While out back, John comes over and joins them in the backyard. Albre catches John up on the events that were to occur on New Year. After they had talked and smoked a couple of blunts. They all go back in the house and eat, and enjoy the leisure time.

Ali and Conan were the first to leave saying they were going back to the traps. John and Gage left shortly after that saying they had business to take care of.

Albre kisses his daughter, and then said his good byes. Then he gives his father his gift, which is a gold Rolex. He accepts the gift his dad bought him, and him and LaToya leave and go back to his apartment in Vaughn Heights. His apartment was furnished now. The delivery truck arriving three days after he moved in. His apartment was decorated nicely but inexpensive. In living room was a leather sofa, love seat and chair with recliner in the corner near the standing lamp, everything was in white with glass coffee and lamps table. One bedroom had a black and gold bedroom set he got from his dad house. In the second bedroom was a water bed and a wood dressers. In the corner was a wooden desk with a brand new Dell computer. In the kitchen area was a gold and glass table to seat four, chairs gold and white.

All in all, he was achieving the urban look quite nicely.

"Trying for the urban look, huh?" LaToya said.

This being her first time visiting since Albre had the apartment.

"Yeah, I think I fail, but hell, I ordered everything off the internet," said Albre.

"Well, you did good, baby. But it could use a woman's touch," said LaToya.

"You welcome to change anything you don't like," said Albre.

Then he gave LaToya her first Christmas present which was the key to his apartment.

"You mean, you giving me the keys to your apartment?" LaToya said. She knew that was a big step for Albre. This meant he couldn't have other girls over. Because LaToya had a key and could come as she pleases.

"Also the key to my heart," said Albre.

He walks into the bedroom and gives LaToya a small jewelry box. She opens it to see a 14-karat gold diamond cut necklace. It has a gold heart filled in with tiny diamonds. LaToya reads the back of the charm. 'I love you, Albre'.

LaToya hugs him, "I love you, too," she said.

"Well, sit down here," said Albre, "there's more to come."

Albre goes into his bedroom, and comes out with a bag. First, he presented her with a 'Tickle Me Elmo' doll, then he gives her a picture of them when they first met at Carnes Park. The picture shows them dancing to the Hot Boyz "Hot Girl". Neither he nor LaToya was looking at the camera. He found out after the concert that Cint had took the picture and he wanted LaToya to have it.

Lastly, he gives her matching earrings, the same shape as the necklace that he had given her. LaToya was elated, and she jumps all over Albre, kissing him, tearing at his clothes.

"Hold up, hold up," said LaToya, "let me give you your gift."

She reaches into her Gucci bag and gives Albre a watch box. When he opens it, it was a black Mavado watch with *"From LaToya"* engraved on the back.

"And for your next present," said LaToya as she strips down to her lingerie.

"Santa must have gotten my list," said Albre.

"And he decided you was a good boy," said LaToya as she kisses him then leads him into the bedroom.

She takes off his shirt then undos his pants. Before he could step out of them, she had him in her mouth. She strokes his manhood, and slob all over it. She pauses for a moment and looks up at him with those "fuck me" eyes. He bits his lips in a display of pleasure then she leads him to the bed. She kisses him all over. Starting at his neck, and ending at his feet. He wiggles and sigh moans of anxiousness. Then she continues to suck on his manhood. When he couldn't take anymore; he rolls her over until he's position on top. He returns all her favors, but more aggressively. He enters her and feels her moistness surrounding his manhood. After they reached ecstasy, he climaxes followed by her shortly afterward.

CHAPTER 20

The Holidays are Almost Over

The holidays were going by fast; school was out so he got to spend more time with LaToya and he didn't have to study for his classes. Just the thought of all the lectures and essays made his brain numb.

Albre was in Brickdale and he and Gage had been slangin, catching all the holiday money which was more than expected. Albre had to double the supply that they kept. Also, he had fiends bringing their kids toys trying to sell their Christmas presents that love ones bought them. He seen it all and when he thought he couldn't see anymore a junkie that he knew had brought his daughter's bicycle trying to sell for some dope. Albre gives him a 20-dollar piece for it and told him that he would shoot his arm off if he came back. Then took the bicycle and gave it back to the junkie's daughter. She was so happy to have her bike; she thought someone had stolen it. Not knowing that the someone was her crack head dad. Her momma thanked Albre and told him that he had a kind heart.

So this particular day while sitting around with Gage,. Albre felt pretty shitty and would be glad when he could put this life behind him.

"You heard from Cash yet?" Gage asked.

"Nah, he and his wife still on vacation," said Albre

"They must have taken a trip around the world," said Gage.
"They won't be back until after New Year," said Albre.

Gage takes out a sack of cocaine and sniffs. Albre notices that Gage have been snorting a lot of cocaine lately. He could see its effect in Gage's face, his face was thinner.

"Hey, man, you need to lay off the cocaine," Albre tells him.

"You know it ain't a habit," said Gage, "it's just to boost me up. You know I be up all time of the night."

"Man, look you need to lay off the cocaine for real," said Albre. Getting angry at his partner in crime.

"Aight, man," said Gage.

"Look, I'll relieve you. You can go do whatever you want. Sleep won't hurt," said Albre.

"Yeah, I do need to go by my girl's house and get some sleep. I doubt if she would want to do much sleeping," said Gage.

They sat around a little while longer. Serving crack heads as they came. They smoke a blunt and Gage leaves. Cint comes walking around the corner.

"Oh, hey Albre," said Cint, "I seen Gage leave, so I came to see what was up with you."

"Gage told me you been stealing dope," said Albre, "damn, Cint."

"Gage lying, I ain't steal shit," said Cint.

"All ya'll crack heads are the same no matter what a nigga do for ya'll," said Albre.

"Albre, look I'm sorry. But Gage don't like to give me dope like you," she said, "hell, he be so high on powder, I'm surprised he noticed."

"Whatever, you steal from me again. I'm gonna cut your ass off, completely," said Albre.

He still gives her some dope because he knows that what she came around for. Gage on the cocaine heavy. Now Cint stealing dope; shit was getting ugly. Albre calls up John while Cint took back off wherever she came from.

"Albre," said John recognizing the number on caller ID.

"Yeah, it's me," said Albre while trying to roll a blunt, "where you at?"

"Oh, I'm out here with Conan in Southlawn," said John.

Conan has been selling weed for John out in Southlawn, ever since Slim OG's gang robbed the spot.

"Well, look, when you get finished out there, come by here, out here in Brickdale," said Albre.

"Aight, about an hour," said John.

"Check," said Albre while hanging up the phone. He fires up the blunt he's been holding while talking to John on the phone.

Ever since Rico got locked up John been moving more and more weed. John was the man, now. He didn't have to go through Cash anymore. Albre really hated being seen with John anymore. Word was the FBI was watching him; they even ran in on him in King Hill but John was tipped off and didn't have any dope. By them letting him go, at least he knew they didn't have him on indictment.

John has been his best friend since forever; and Albre needs to talk to him because he knew John would understand.

When John turned the corner, Albre could hear him coming. His Impala had floor mats that made it sound heavy. Albre and John goes in the house as not to be seen. Albre tells John about Gage on the powder strong, about Cint stealing from them, and about him wanting to get out the game.

"It ain't for me man," said Albre.

"What you gonna do? Just drop everything. Then what?" John asked, "you know I can't tell you what to do. But if I were you, I would stay in until I graduated."

"Yeah, that was my plan. But the way things been going, I'm having second thoughts, man. I got a daughter," Albre tells him, rolling up another blunt.

John can tell he's nervous. He's been knowing Albre since they moved to the Gump.

"Whenever you ready to leave the game, I got your back. Just think about it first," John tells him.

CHAPTER 21

New Years Eve

At eight p.m. on New Years Eve, a room was purchased at Red Carpet Inn, on the West South Boulevard. Inside sat five black men dressed in black. Two of them had sawed off shotguns; one had an AK-47, and the other a tech nine. The last one had two nine-millimeter Berettas.

"Look, we take them coming out the house," said Albre.

"My source tells me they just arrived and in the house now," said John.

"Is that's all of them?" Gage asked.

"Yeah, and Slim OG with them," said John.

"Slim OG is caution, so he probably will be the last one out," said Albre.

"Aim to kill, because they will retaliate if we fuck up," said John.

"Any questions?" Albre asked, "everyone knows what to do?"

Everyone nods in agreement. The two youngest one didn't say anything the entire meeting. It was their first time in the battlefield.

"You aight Conan?" Albre asked.

"Yeah, I'm cool," said Conan.

"What about you, Ali?" Albre asked.

"I'm good, just butterflies in my stomach," Ali said.

"Here, hit this," said John as he passes the cocaine.

At exactly 9:22 p.m., a blue Ford Station Wagon driven by John approached a house at 137 Mason Avenue, coming out the house was nine black men, most of them with red bandannas tied around them some place, and Slim OG was the last to leave the house. As he steps outside, he sees the blue station wagon with its headlights off. In the Station Wagon driven by John, Albre hangs out the front passenger window with two nine-millimeter Berettas. One in each hand. Conan is out the back passenger window with the sawed off shotgun. Ali is standing up leaning out the back driver's window facing the tailgate with the AK-47.

When Slim OG and his gang see this, some try to retreat hack into the house. Some dive behind cars. Slim OG didn't make it because Albre has such an accurate shot. He was shot two times in the chest, and once in the leg. Six other members of Slim OG's gang were shot. Four of those members died, and two were critically injured.

The Station Wagon with Albre and his click hanging out the windows speed off. Gage still unloading the AK-47 from the tailgate. John pulls the Station Wagon up at the convenient store on the other side of town. Albre and everyone else leaves their masks, shirts, and guns in the Station Wagon. Then they get in the rented Honda Accord and go back to the hotel room. John takes the Station Wagon. First, he disposed of the guns, and then he takes the Station Wagon to the country. He wipes the car down to get rid of fingerprints, and then he gets in the other rented Honda Accord he parks there earlier.

Once he reached the city, he heads for the Red Carpet Inn when everyone was at the room accounted for and not injured. Adrenaline was still rushing through their veins. They smoke a couple of blunts, and then they all piled in Albre's suburban to go to Dake's Pool Hall. They celebrated the New Year at Dake Pool Hall, drinking and smoking blunt after blunt that was their alibi for New Year Eve.

CHAPTER 22

January...Events after the New Year

After the events on New Year, Conan and Gage was catching some heat from the homicide SWAT. Since their alibi was air tight, soon everything died down. Now everything was back to normal. Cash was back off vacation. Well, everything was almost back to normal. The Roc was still getting twenty percent and this had to stop ASAP.

Everyone was pointing finger at the Roc for the drive by that killed Slim OG and four of his gang member. The ones that were injured and survived recognized the blue station wagon. It was believed to have been spotted at the Roc safehouse before the shooting. Of course, Albre paid to have this information circulating; also, John threw gasoline on this fire. He had someone say they seen one of the Roc boys ditched the car.

So now, the heat was on the Roc. Slim OG surviving game members were feed info to believe the Roc was behind the shooting and who was the wiser. Albre could pay the Roc twenty percent because everything would run its course soon.

CHAPTER 23

LaToya's Senior Prom

Back at his apartment in Vaughn Heights, LaToya and Albre sits around talking. Albre had been studying for his final exam, which was in a month and a half. He would graduate from Alabama State in May with his Bachelor Degree in Business management. LaToya would graduate from high school.

LaToya had been looking for a dress to wear to her senior prom. She had been begging him to go along with her for two months now. Finally, he accepted, because he didn't want her to go to the prom alone. This was one event Albre dreaded because he knew he would probably be the oldest person there and hell, he had missed his own senior prom. He wasn't into the prom thing. At his own senior prom, everyone expected him to be there because he was so popular; he just decided not to show up at all. So he was seeing Shonta, and then she had just recently given birth to his daughter. However, he really loved LaToya, so he couldn't deny her the experience that was one of the greatest memorable moment of high school. In addition, he would most definitely make it the night of her life. He had told her while she was selecting her dress to getting any one that she wanted, no matter how much it cost.

Albre was tired because he had recently returned from another trip to Atlanta. Where he had took 190 thousand dollars and placed in the safe deposit box along with the money he already had. He had a substantial amount in his stash and he could up and leave right now and have enough money to live comfortably.

"Hey, baby, I'm tired of this life style," Albre tells LaToya as he lays his head on her lap.

"What are you going to do about it?" she asked.

"Well, I was thinking if you want that when you graduate from high school, and I graduate from Alabama State; we could relocate somewhere and start all over. You could go to college if you want and I can start my business. Because I mean, I don't want to live my life worrying about get busted with dope and going to prison or getting shot and killed. I don't want to have to look over my shoulder everyday like I don't know," said Albre.

LaToya just rubs his shoulders as he closes his eyes and talks to her. She knows Albre is a good man and she really loves him.

"I mean when I got into this game, I just wanted to make some money and get out and now it's like I can't," Albre stops to look into her eyes with sincerity, "and you are so young, I don't want anything to happen to you or Shonta or Bre."

LaToya looks into his eyes and said, "Albre, you know I love you. So whatever you decide, I'm behind you one hundred percent. I'm your down ass bitch, man."

She leans down and gives him a kiss. That kiss was returned with a kiss from him, followed by another more passionate kiss. Soon, they were in the guest bedroom. He stood behind her kissing on her neck, caressing her breasts. She moans in anticipation. He pulls her shirt over her head, and then he undoes her brassiere. He turns her around to face him, and as they both stand in the room half-naked. He licks on her exposed breast, kissing and licking on her sides. She grabs her head from excitement and starts pulling her hair. He unbuttons her pants and she wiggles out of them until they fall down to the floor. He eagerly undresses himself, and then lays her down on the waterbed. She tensed up at first because the waterbed was cool.

He stands for a minute to devour the view of her body. She's so beautiful. Honey bun complexioned skin, not a bruise or mark on her body, and curves in all the right places. Her breasts are perfectly round and small. He licks his lips then starts to lavish kisses on her, starting with her feet, and before long, he had reached her treasures. There he licked and sucks, tasting all of her juices. She arches her back from pleasure. When she reached her first climax. Then and only then did he place his throbbing man hood inside her. Inside the warm wetness of her, he came.

CHAPTER 24

Drug Surveillance

At the Peddler's Inn, the Montgomery Police Department Drug Task Force has set up surveillance. These were undercover detectives assigned to watch the activities at one of the busiest dope traps on the Southwest Side. They had established surveillance in room 222. They had a perfect view to watch the young men in room 101 and 102. The detectives also had a room on the backside because they knew through an informant that the group of young men changes side every other week.

Ali and Rick were up to the usual in room 102. Today they had the dope stash in a hole in the wall in the adjoining room, room 101. Rick was playing the PlayStation. Ali was sitting at the table counting money, waiting for Gage to make his round and pick up the money. It was 6 p.m. and the pickup time changed every day.

A car horn blows; Ali peeks out the window and sees that it was Gage in his Buick.

"Hey, Gage's here," Ali tells Rick.

Rick stops playing the PlayStation and grabs his .380 semi-automatic handgun and lets Ali out the door. Rick watches closely as Ali gets in the car with Gage and they drive off. Five minutes later Gage's car returns and drops Ali off at the room.

Unaware of the surveillance in room 222. These types of activities carry on for a couple more days. Then the young men change room and were now on the backside of the hotel. This time they were in rooms 113 and 114.

The undercover detectives reserved rooms of the same hotel so they could watch these rooms for they were aware of the young men's routine. They knew exactly what to watch and where to be. The undercover detectives already had enough evidence now to get a search warrant and burst in the hotel rooms the two young men occupied. But they still hadn't seen the young man they were assigned to get evidence of drug dealing. They knew who the young man was who came around every morning and night in the 1990 Buick LeSable.

According to the information they got when they ran his car tag; his name was Gabriel Pool, and they assume he was dropping off dope and picking up money. They had seen him before when they were watching the apartment in Smiley Court. That when the young man with the dreads made out the old beat up green van they had surveillance set up in and closed down the trap. According to their informant, the young man with the dreads was supposedly to be the same person running this trap at the Inn and several others around the Southside. They only knew his face and he goes by the name of Albre. This is who they were assigned to, but for some reason he hasn't been seen around the hotel room lately.

The Montgomery Police Department Drug Task Force was on a tight leash, and even tighter budget if they didn't make out on their assignment. They would have to end their surveillance. Unless their superior wanted to burst the hotel room anyway. Regardless, they only had three more days of surveillance, and they were hoping this Albre would show up and give them a reason that their superior would extend their surveillance.

CHAPTER 25

Albre Meets with His Father

Albre has been spending two hundred thousand at a time with Cash. He was buying twelve bricks at a time, and because he was buying so many, Cash was letting him get them for sixteen thousand a brick. But, Albre felt he should be getting them for at least fourteen five. So one afternoon, after classes, Albre drives over to Top Knotch Jewelry and talks to Cash.

"What's up, Albre?" Cash asked as Albre walks in his office.

"Look, man, we've been doing good business for a minute now; and I've been buying twelve or more Rolexes at a time," said Albre.

He was referring to kilo as Rolexes in case the office was bugged. That's the way they always talk in a place that could be bugged and Cash's office is most definitely at the top of the list of places that could be bugged.

"Yeah, you have been making me mad money, young man," said Cash as he sits his 300-pound frame behind his desk.

"Well, at sixteen a piece, I'm not seeing no money, because I'm having to employ more people, plus I'm still breaking the Roc of twenty percent of all profits," Albre tells Cash with a straight face.

He is thinking to himself that the Roc has to be taking care of for it doesn't look like Slim OG gang went for the bait they left to make it look like the Roc had Slim OG killed. It has been months and they haven't retaliated on the Roc yet.

"So you suggesting that I drop the price?" Cash voice brings Albre out of his thoughts.

"Yeah, I know you good people. So that's why I came to you," said Albre to him.

"Shit, Albre, you putting me in a fucked up predicament. But since I like you, and I see a lot of potential in you, I'm gonna do you a favor. I'm gonna talk to my people and see do he want to meet you. Because the prices you talking about, hell, I can't do it," said Cash he pauses to read Albre facial expression, "if he wants to talk to you or meet you, I'll call you."

"Aight, see what you can make happen," said Albre as he reaches out to shake Cash's hand.

Cash stands up and shakes his hand from behind that big mahogany desk. Then he escorts Albre out.

Once outside and in his truck, Albre thinks over the conversation, and something's not right. Cash is gonna introduce Albre to the connection. Then that cuts Cash out completely. Albre knows Cash is not going to miss out on all the money that he is making from him that easily. So Albre knows something definitely doesn't smell right, so now he got to watch Cash.

In the meantime, his payment of two hundred thousand to Cash isn't going to stop, because he needs his dope supply to keep flowing.

Albre goes by his dad's house. He sees his dad's truck parked out front. He was tempted to keep on going because he knew his dad has some words for him, but he stops and goes in.

"Yo, what's up, Dad?" Albre said to his father.

"Yeah, like you care, the way you been avoiding me," his father replies.

"Damn, Dad, I haven't been avoiding you. It's just that I got final exams, graduation, and stuff coming up. I've been busy," said Albre.

"Yeah, but you still selling them drugs," his father said to him as he was walking into the living room where he sits back down.

Albre notices that his dad was watching the news, so he sits down and watches the news with his father. Because he knows his dad loves him and he needs to reassure him that he does planned to make a legitimate life for himself. They watch the local news in silent and all the news reports had to talk about was the killing, robbing, and drugs like that was all that took place in Montgomery. But, that's all the news reporter talked about. When the local news went off and the ABC World News started coming on that's when his father turned the TV off.

"Son, you know how much your mother and I wanted to see you go to college like your brother," said his dad, "I'm glad your mother's not alive to see you now. But I know she's turning over in her grave." Albre listens to his dad, blinking his eyes fast to fight back tears.

"I love you, son. But you know I didn't raise you to run them streets and be out there selling drugs. I don't want you to make the same mistakes I made and end up in prison. Boy, God seen fit for to let me out of prison so I could do right by you and your brother. When I got out I change my life, I couldn't end up dead or go back to prison, I didn't want ya'll growing up without a mother and a father," he pauses to let his words sink in. "Your brother went to college on your mother's death insurance money. He got that expensive degree, now he's letting it go to waste. He wants to run a damn club and launder money. But I just knew you would do better. You got a beautiful daughter and a chance to do right by her. To give her a good life. Son, I'm not telling you how to live your life. I'm gonna love you the same. But I wanted you to go to college so you could be anything you want to be. Not be one of these niggers that's always talking about the white man this, the white man that. They use that as their excuses to do nothing. I wanted you to have an education, so you could get as far as the white man in this world. We already at a disadvantage because we're black. You can make a lot of money the right way. The way you use to tell me how you wanted your own business."

"Tell me, son, do you love me?" Albre's father asked him.

"Dad, you know I love you," Albre tells his dad.

"Then, son, promise me that I won't lose you to the streets. I don't want to have to bury you beside your mother," his father says to him with tears in his eyes.

"Dad, I promise when I graduate next month, I'm gonna leave the streets alone," said Albre.

"Whatever you do, I'm gonna be here for you, okay? Just be careful," his father said.

"I love you, Dad," said Albre.

He embraces his father. They talk a little while longer and Albre leaves his dad's house.

CHAPTER 26

Search and Serizure Warrent

Albre leaves school early because he has just gotten word from his source inside the police department that the Drug Task Force has had the Peddler's Inn under surveillance for a week and they had just obtain a search and seizure warrant. The warrant was to be carried out as soon as all the Task Force members were assembled. Which should take about an hour according to his source.

Albre knew he didn't have time to waste so he placed a call to Gage on his cell..

"Where you at?" he asked Gage.

"I'm in Brickdale with Cint. She cooking some yams," Gage responds.

"I'm on my way out there. Tell Cint I'm not hungry," said Albre as he ends the call so he can fight traffic.

Albre knew Gage was referring to dope as yams and told him he wasn't hungry, so Cint could stop cooking the dope. Before Albre reaches Brickdale, he stops by a gas station and uses the pay phone to call Ali's cell phone.

"What's poppin'?" Ali answers on the first ring.

Albre says, "Make like an egg and beat it." Ali immediately recognizes the voice on the other end as Albre.

"Now, man, flush all that shit and get out," Albre tells him as his hearts beats 100 times per second.

The phone went dead and Albre hears a dial tone. He gets back in his truck and continues on to Brickdale.

The atmosphere at the room was ecstatic. As Ali stuff the money in a backpack while Rick and two other niggas emptied bag after bag of dope and flush it down the toilet. It was so much dope by it being the early part of the day that they had to use the toilet in reach room. After they flush all the dope, Ali gives the back pack to Lil' Troy. The youngest of the group and sends him walking to the hotel across the street.

Ali and the other two young men wait ten minutes after Lil' Troy leaves, before they all exited out the room. When they were pulling out the parking lot, Ali Cadillac was blocked by a black on black Suburban and a van scoop in on the hotel rooms. Four Drug Task Force Officers jumped out of the black Suburban that had them blocked in and handcuffed them. Seven other Drug Task Force Officers rallied the two hotel rooms to find them clean and unoccupied. Ali, Rick, and Man were all handcuffed and placed in separate squad patrol cars that had arrived on the scene. The two undercover detectives who had obtained the warrant were unhappy to find the two rooms clean. They knew their superior was not going to be happy if they came up empty handed. So one of the detectives plants two ounce of cocaine in the hotel room behind the desk and the other detective plants a 9mm handgun in Ali's Cadillac.

Detective Warren, the heaviest of the two detectives, approaches the squad car that Ali was in.

"Whose pistol is that in your car?" he asked Ali.

"What pistol?" Ali asked.

"A black 9mm," the detective tells him.

"It wasn't no pistol in my car!" Ali said to him thinking he was set up.

"Yeah, what's this?" Detective Warren produces the handgun inside a Ziploc bag.

"That wasn't in my car," said Ali.

"Well, you're under arrest, you punk bitch. Someone read him his right," the detective barks as he walks off.

Detective Dunlap, the skinny detective, repeat this same scheme about the two ounces of cocaine to Rick. But Rick denies the dope and immediately knew the dope had been planted. In addition, Man denied knowing about both the dope and the gun. So they all were taken down to the police station.

Albre was in Brickdale, waiting impatiently on Ali to call him back. After two hours had passed, Lil' Troy called Gage cell phone.

"Hey, they got Ali and them," Lil' Troy talks into the phone breathlessly.

"Wait, slow down lil' nigga. Where you at?" Gage asked.

Lil' Troy tells him he's at the Red Carpet Inn across the street from the Peddler's Inn. He gives him the room number.

Gage and Albre go to pick up Lil' Troy in his smoke gray Suburban. After they pick him up, he began telling them what had happened while they return to Brickdale.

"So when you left with the money and pistols in the backpack, they were supposed to give you a couple of minutes and they were all gonna leave in Ali's car," Albre asked him when they arrived in Brickdale.

"Yeah, but when I leave. Before I could make it all the way across the street, Task Force boys had blocked Ali's car in, and jumped out on them," said Lil' Troy.

"Then what happened?" Albre asked.

"I was trying not to be spotted. But I seen them put Ali, Rick, and Man in the back of the police squad cars," he said.

They all get out of Gage's truck and go inside the house in Brickdale. Cint is sitting at the table smoking a cigarette. Gage informs her on what happened at the Peddler's Inn. Albre sits beside Lil' Troy rolling a blunt.

"You sure they flushed all the dope?" he asked.

"I helped them flush the dope, so I'm positive," responds Lil' Troy.

"How much money is in the backpack?" Albre asked.

"I don't know," he answers.

"Cint counts that money," Albre instructs Cint.

Cint grabs the backpack off the table and starts to count the bills inside. Albre sits back on the couch gathering his thoughts. Then he calls John and Conan out in Southlawn and tells them to come to Brickdale. He decides he would wait until they get there to tell them what had happened. Once Cint get through counting the money, she comes up with $38,700. She recounts the money before telling Albre how much.

"Cint, could you please get a phone book and look up Johnny Whitlock, criminal defense lawyer," Albre asked her, "once you find the phone number, call him and setup an appointment for this evening before his office closes. Tell him it's an emergency."

Cint does what she was asked and confirms an appointment for 4 p.m. She tells Albre of his appointment time, and writes down the address for him.

"That's in an hour," Cint tells Albre.

Albre gets the money and gets ready to leave when John and Conan pull up out in front.

"Say, Albre, what's going on?" John asked as he and Conan enters the house.

"When I was at school, I got a call saying the Drug Task Force was about to run in on Ali and Rick at the Peddler's Inn, so I left school then call Ali and tell him to flush the dope and get the hell out," Albre continues, "Ali sent Lil' Troy across the street with the money and pistols. But before they could leave the Task force pulled up on them. Now, Ali, Rick, and Man are down at the police station. Lil' Troy got away with the money."

John and Conan look shocked as Albre reveals this information to them.

"They was clean, right?" John asked Lil' Toy.

Albre interrupts, "Yeah, they flushed all the dope. So they should have been clean. But they still got taken down to the police station. I don't know what's going on so I had Cint setup an appointment with that lawyer you used. I'm about to go see him now."

"Well, I'm going with you. Mr. Whitlock will go down to the police station and see what is going on," John reassures Albre.

"Aight, let's go then. Everyone else stay here. Gage, hold the spot down," Albre tells him as they leave.

CHAPTER 27

Mr. Whitlock

"Mr. Whitlock will see you now," a blonde haired, white woman in her early thirties tells them.

She gets up to lead Albre and John into the lawyer's office.

"Hello, Mr. Warren," the tall white man, with the military haircut said in recognizing John.

They exchanged handshakes.

"And you must be Mr. Jackson?" asked the lawyer.

"I am," replies Albre.

"What can I do for you gentlemen?" the lawyer asked as he offers them seats.

They take their seats and Mr. Whitlock returns to his huge brown leather recliner behind his even bigger antique oak wood desk. Albre takes in the atmosphere of this exquisite office. Expensive paintings hung from the walls, antique artifacts sits on top of the big oak wood desk. A computer is to the right of the desk, on a smaller desk. Bookshelves lined the walls behind them containing legal books, criminal digest and supreme courts cases. Various awards hung the wall, and sat atop the shelves. Directly behind the lawyer was a breathtaking view of downtown Montgomery and the Riverfront of Alabama River.

Albre was brought back to reality by a bump from John.

"Oh, yeah, Mr. Whitlock, my friends were arrested a couple of hours ago by the Montgomery Police Department Drug Task Force. I assume they were arrested, because they were handcuffed and taken down to the police station," Albre continues as the lawyer listens attentively, "they were at the Peddler's Inn, getting ready to leave when the Task Force agents jumped out on them."

"Obviously, the DTF presumed they were selling drug out of the room," the lawyer interrupts.

"Right, anyway, I'm sure there isn't any drugs in the room," Albre states.

"Okay, then what do you want from me?" asked the lawyer. *Smart ass, Albre thought to himself.*

John intervenes, "Look, we want you to go down to the police station and represent our friends. Before the narcotics detectives gets to feeling themselves. You know what I mean?"

"I need more information on this and there's a retainer fee," the lawyer said.

Albre cuts the lawyer off by setting the backpack on the desk.

"Thirty eight thousand and seven hundred dollars," said Albre.

"That should take care of all the expenses for now," said the lawyer.

"They might not be under arrest for anything. They could just be down there for questioning," said the lawyer.

"Whatever the case may be, if they are under arrest. Get them a bond and let me know. Just make your presence known and assure my friends that you will take care of them," said Albre.

"I'm on my way down to the police station as soon as we're done here," said the lawyer.

They shake hands again, Albre writes down the names for the lawyer and they leave.

"Mr. Jackson, my secretary will write you a receipt on your way out. Good day, gentlemen," said the lawyer.

After they arrive back in Brickdale, everyone was pretty much at ease, knowing Albre had obtain a lawyer to go see about Ali, Rick, and Man.

Cint wasn't her usual self. She was more nervous, chain-smoking Newport's 100s back to back. Gage, Conan, and Lil' Troy had been snorting cocaine so they were paranoid. Albre and John go in the kitchen and talks.

"That was really close, John. It could have been anyone of the traps. Hell, I could have been there. The only reason I wasn't around lately was that I've been having a lot going on with these final exams next week," Albre tells John.

"Look, shit like this happens. That's why you pay ole girl at the police station. It's part of the game," said John to him.

"Well, I'm through with the game. I can't take this shit. I'm gonna let Gage have all this shit for himself," he said.

"You know whatever you decide, I got your back. You my nigga," said John.

He hugs Albre to show him some love.

"But right now, I'm about to bounce," John tells him as he leaves.

Albre goes back in the living room where everyone is at and tells them it's a change of plans.

"Cint, you and Lil' Troy go open back up the trap at your apartment in Smiley Court. Gage you hold this spot here down. Conan, you be about busy as usual in Southlawn," he tells them.

"Ya'll know we got to keep shit going we got the whole Souhtside looking at us now. Trying to see if we gonna get scared," said Albre. He speaks with authority in his voice. "plus, we got all this dope that Cint about to cook up we get to get rid of,"

"Everybody straight?" Albre asked looking in each face for signs of insecurities and then continues, "aight, ya'll keep ya'll phones on. I'm out. I'm tired as hell. If Ali, Rick, or Man calls one of ya'll phones. Hit me up," Albre told them before he left.

CHAPTER 28

Things Were Back to Usual

Things were back to usual, Ali, Rick, and Man was each out on personal recognition bond. Thanks to Mr. Whitlock. Ali was charged with possession of stolen firearm. Rick and Man were charged with possession of cocaine with intent to distribute. Mr. Whitlock didn't think they were going to get indicted on the charges. Since it looked like some desperate crump up charges.

Cint and Lil' Troy were booming in Smiley Court. Conan was out in Soutlawn with John around every now and then. Gage had shit on locked in Brickdale. Ali and Rick were back to selling dope. But they had established a spot on the corner in Brickdale and was only nickels and dimes.

Albre was on his way to meet Cash. Cash had told him that his connect wanted to meet him in two weeks. That when he would be in town from Florida. Albre arrives at Top Knotch Jewelry and goes to the back where Cash's office is located. Cash meets him at the door and greets him.

"How you doing, young man?" Cash embraces him.

"I'm good," said Albre.

"Look, I have received this week's shipment," Albre told him, not one for small talk.

"I haven't received last week's payment," responds Cash.

"Like I told you, one of our spot got busted up and we took a lost. I was gonna make payment double this week," he tells Cash.

"Well, we all take risk in this business. If your spot got knocked, then that means they must be watching you," said Cash.

"Naw, I don't be around like that. I'm a behind-the-scenes type of guy now. My source tells me they bust the Inn because it's been a lot of drug activities there lately," said Albre lying about what his source inside the MPD told him.

"Your drugs," said Cash.

"Naw, your drugs," responds Albre with a look of sarcasm.

"Anyway, since Slim OG got killed, and you still paying the Roc twenty percent. A lot of young guys been trying to establish themselves on the Southside. But that's just talk," said Cash.

"Yeah, well, that talk means they don't fear us enough," asserts Albre.

"So what you gonna do about it?" Cash asked him.

"I'm gone take care of the rumors. I wish a nigga would think about challenging me on the Southside," Albre tells him.

"I'm gonna let you have this dope, young man. But it's not gonna be at the U-Storage-it. It's at E-Z-Store-it," said Cash.

Then he wrote down the information and hands him a key.

"It's gonna be here from now on out. Unless I tell you otherwise. But handle your business and keep my money coming," said Cash.

As Cash tells him, he spins around in his leather chair, giving Albre his back that means he is through with the conversation.

Outside of Top Knotch Albre gets in his '89 butter scotch candy Suburban and leaves, heading for E-Z storage. He takes unnecessary rout leaving out the city to assure he's not being followed. Cash always keeping dope in storage outside the city. Albre thinks to himself as he drives on I-85 toward Shorter, Alabama.

When he arrived in Shorter, he had no problem finding the E-Z-Store-it. As small, as the town was he was surprise they had an E-Z-Store it. After he had loaded the drugs in the truck. Albre made a mental note not to drive his truck back down to Shorter because his truck was too flashy and might draw attention in this country town.

Once on the road again, he went to thinking of a way to get the Roc out of his pocket because he was tired of paying him twenty percent and he needed to make a statement for anyone thinking of selling dope on his territory. The Southside was his territory now. Once inside the city limits, he decided that he would put a hit out on the Roc amongst his own click and gives fifty thousand dollars to the one that cashes I on his head. Besides, he was just trying to maintain until after his graduation. Then he would leave everything to Gage and the fellows. Until then, he had to make it look like he was the man. He was in control.

Albre picks Cint up from Smiley Court, and takes her and drops her off in Brickdale, so she could cook up the dope. Before departing, he tells Gage to put word out amongst the gang that there was a fifty-thousand-dollar-price on the Roc's head.

CHAPTER 29

Albre at His Dads...Then Off to the Prom

"Daddy, Daddy, you look handsome," Bre tells Albre.

Albre was at his dad's house in Ridgecrest getting ready to pick up LaToya and take her to her senior prom. His father and Janice were keeping Bre for the weekend.

"Thank you, princess," said Albre.

Albre leans down and kisses his daughter.

"Can I go with you, Daddy?" Bre asked him.

"Not this time, Princess. You are not old enough to fit your glass slipper," he tells his daughter playfully, referring to Cinderella.

"Dad, can you help me with this tie?" Albre asked his father.

"How you do on your exams?" asked his father.

"I won't know until next week, but I felt like I did good," Albre tells him.

He had taken his final exams early in the week and he was stressed waiting for the results. All in all, he knew he passed. They weren't really a challenge to him because he had been studying hard.

"In that case, I know you aced them," his father told him.

"Boy, what possessed you to buy that damn car? That could have been money you spend on a house," said his father.

"Aw Pops! You now you like the car. You're jealous that's all," said Albre.

He had just brought a brand new dark blue 2000 Lexus convertible yesterday; and went to have a set of 20" chrome Ashanti rims with P-Zero's tire put on the same day. It was LaToya's graduation gift; she hasn't seen it yet. So he was going to present it to her tonight. Plus, he felt guilty for not spending that much time with her lately.

"I just might trade in the Cadillac for one of those. It might be too small for me, though," his father said putting the finishing touches on Albre bow tie.

"Well, baby girl, come give daddy a hug," said Albre.

Bre runs to give her daddy a big hug and a kiss.

"Hurry home before your car turns into a pumpkin," said Bre referring again to the Cinderella story.

"Oh, that car better not turn into a pumpkin. Daddy paid too much money for that car," said Albre before he leaves.

"Don't forget your carnation," Janice, his dad's girlfriend, tells him before he exits the door.

He returns to get the carnation out of the refrigerator. Damn, why couldn't things been like this when it was time to go to his own prom. He didn't go because he was having problems with his baby momma, Shonta during that time, and Bre was only a couple of months old.

As Albre enters Smiley Court, he is tempted to stop by Cint's apartment and check on the trap. He remembers this is LaToya night, besides he had checked in with everyone and told them he could he reached on his cell phone. Having thoughts of his cell phone, he reaches in the jacket of his tuxedo and turns off his phone. They'll have to leave a message, he said to himself. This is LaToya's night.

So when he arrives in front of LaToya's apartment in the newly purchased Lexus convertible. He gets out and goes to the door. Before he could knock, it swings open.

"Hey, Albre," LaToya's mother, Ms. Kay greets him.

"How you doing, Ms. Kay. Is LaToya ready?" Albre asked.

"She'll be down in a minute. Come on in. You look really nice, Albre," Ms. Kay tells him.

"Thank you," said Albre.

"Toya!," calls Ms. Kay upstairs for her daughter, "Albre's here."

"That girl has been driving me crazy all day. Momma this, momma that. Hell, she probably still ain't ready," said Ms. Kay.

LaToya's mother is like the typical black woman with a five kids, and their father has abandoned them. Ms. Kay works a regular job. She has five kids, LaToya being the oldest. She is another black woman trying to beat the odds and Ms. Kay doing a pretty good job at it. Even though she lives in Smiley Court, you couldn't tell by the way her house is kept. She is to be commended for having five kids in a three-bedroom apartment that she keeps clean, cool, and nicely decorated. LaToya recently told him, Ms. Kay was moving into her own home next month, once the bank approves the loan. Albre decided he would help with that. Especially since her oldest daughter will be graduating from high school, and moving out soon. Even though she was happy for her daughter's accomplishments, she would really miss LaToya. However, she would only have four kids to take care of instead of five.

"Hey, Albre," said LaToya.

He turns around to see LaToya standing at the bottom of the stairs. She was stunningly beautiful in a light blue Vera Wang evening gown with the

V-neck line that partially exposes her breasts and it gracefully hugged the curves of her body. She had her hair pinned up on her head in a sort of French roll with a band with steaks of blue coming down the left side of her face, but barely covers her left eye. She sported a diamond studded earing and matching diamond necklace that Albre had bought for her. She was the perfect picture of a black Cinderella; she even had on four-inch glass Jimmy Choo heels.

"LaToya, you look beautiful," said Albre as he finally broke the silent.

"And you look very handsome yourself, Mr. Jackson," said LaToya as she smiles at him.

Her smile took his breath away; he knew that he love this girl.

"Mama, what's wrong?" LaToya asked when she finally recognizes her mother was crying.

"Oh, nothing, baby. You just look so beautiful," said Ms. Kay to her daughter, "oh, let me get my camera."

"Here's your carnation," Albre tells LaToya, still drunk by the sight of his beautiful date.

"Okay, Okay. Let me get some pictures," said Ms. Kay as she runs back in with a Polaroid camera.

"Okay, you two, big smiles," said Ms. Kay as she takes picture after picture. Then she runs out of film.

"Here, use my camera," Albre tells her and produces his digital camera.

After about twenty pictures on the digital camera, some together, and some alone. They were ready to go. Ms. Kay followed them to the door and watch as they walked to the Lexus.

"Damn, Albre you bought a new car?" LaToya asked.

"Yeah, and it's yours. Happy early graduation!" he tells her.

"Oh my gawd, oh my gawd," LaToya screams, tears running down her eyes. "Mama, Albre brought me a car. He bought me a Lexus!"

She hugs Albre then runs to the car and looks inside. Nosy neighbors who are out sitting on their porches as they do in every project, watch with curiosity. Albre and Ms. Kay walks out to the car and LaToya was all over it.

"Ya'll have fun," Ms. Kay tells them.

"We will and I'll take care of her," said Albre then he looks at LaToya,

"I'll be your chauffer tonight, Cinderella. Shall we leave?" Albre said.

"We shall," responds LaToya.

And they were off to the prom.

CHAPTER 30

At the Prom

They arrived to a packed parking lot at the Montgomery Civic Center that hosted George Washington Carver High School Prom. The prom started at 7 p.m., and it was 7:30 when Albre pulled the Lexus up in front of the Civic Center. As Albre anticipated, their entrance was noticed because he could see everyone looking through the window at them as he and LaToya exited the car.

Albre door was open by a valet attendant and he gave the guy the keys and he walks around to the passenger side and opens the door for LaToya. LaToya had reapplied her makeup, because she was looking blemished after crying.

"Are you ready, Cinderella?" Albre asked her.

"Yes," was her only reply.

She grabs his arm and he leads her through the glass door to her senior prom. When they walked through the door, all eyes were on them. They could see camera lights flashing around them. They felt like celebrities, and they look the part too.

Once they were inside and the commotion that their late entrance had come to cease. They walked around together, LaToya mingled with her friends a little but she never strayed far from Albre. Afraid one of her little girlfriends might try to make advances on him!

"Well, you sure deserve it," said Albre looking around the room.

LaToya was very popular at school, this he knew. Now, looking at all the rest of the young ladies, he could see why. There were some beautiful young ladies in the room and well dressed in expensive gowns, but LaToya was by far the most beautiful and most expensively dressed, he was sure, knowing that the Vera Wang dress she was wearing cost three thousand dollars. Hell, both of her younger sisters could wear that dress when it was their time to go to their senior prom!

"Let's go take your prom pictures," he suggests to LaToya, "before we start dancing."

They go and take the picture in a white on gray backdrop with the "One in an Million" logo.

"Come on Albre, this is my song," said LaToya as she drags him towards the center of the dance floor.

As Usher's voice filled the room with his hit single, "You Got it Bad." And Albre being not a bad dancer really enjoys himself. Then the music breaks, and some woman were on the stage getting ready to announce the prom king and queen.

LaToya holds Albre tight as the woman was saying, "And your prom queen is...LaToya Knight!"

"Ahhh," LaToya screams, then kisses Albre and runs awkwardly in those glasses heels towards the stage.

When on the stage, the woman places a crown on LaToya's head and gives her a bouquet of roses. Then the woman announces the prom king:

"And your prom king is," the woman pauses for anticipation, "Stephen Hill."

And some guy enters the stage, the woman presents him with a crown and a cane.

"A few words from out prom queen," the woman said.

LaToya steps up to the microphone with her biggest smile and said, "I love you Classmates, oh my gawd. I'm so glad to be a part of this class. It has been fun. Thank you all and thanks to my boyfriend, Albre," she screams and then continues, "this has been the best night of my life. Thank you all."

Stephen gets up to the microphones and he said two or three words of thanks, and then he and LaToya take pictures together in front of the camera. Then they were led to the front where they dance to a Maxwell song. Half way through the song Albre taps Stephen on the shoulder.

"May I cut in?" Albre asked.

"Sure," Stephen said and walked away.

"LaToya, you're glowing," Albre tells her.

"This is the best night of my life, Albre. I love you," said LaToya.

"I love you, too," answers Albre.

And thirty minutes later they said their good byes and left early.

Once inside the car, Albre checks his phone for messages; and to his surprise, he had none.

"You know there's an after party at the Ramada," said LaToya.

"Yeah, after dinner. I got your after party," Albre smiled and LaToya smiled back.

They went and had an expensive dinner at a restaurant called "Martin's" where you can only get a table with reservation. Albre had made reservation a week earlier for one of the most expensive tables in the house. They were all expensive at the restaurant. Albre orders a 1951 bottle of Chardonnay, and he eats lobster and salad. One they were full and tipsy from the Chardonnay, they leave and Albre tips the waiter handsomely. When they left the restaurant, it was 11 p.m.

"So where to now, Sir Romeo?" LaToya asked while enjoying the night.

"The night is still young, Cinderella, and your coach don't turn into a pumpkin until midnight," jokes Albre.

"But we should be safe by then. Because I got us a room at the La Quinta Inn," said Albre.

When they got to the La Quinta, the white woman greets Albre with a smug expression.

"May I help you?" asked the receptionist with a tone that said surely these black people are out of place.

"Miles Jackson. We have a reservation," Albre speak matter of factly.

The white woman types on the keyboard and said, "Yes, Mr. Jackson. Can I see some ID, please? Just for verification."

Like she needs to explain herself. Albre looks at LaToya who wants to something, and then he gives the woman his ID.

The white woman studies the ID, then says to Albre, "Um, yes, sorry about that Mr. Jackson. Your room is on the top floor. Room 902, the Presidential Suite." Then she handed Albre the key.

"Thanks," said Albre and then he smiles and leads LaToya to the elevator.

"Bitch!" said LaToya on the elevator.

They both laugh and then Albre kisses her. When the doors opened on the ninth floor, they were still kissing. Once inside the Presidential Suite, Albre put a *"Do Not Disturb"* sign on the outside of the doorknob and close the door. When he turns around, LaToya smiles and let her three-thousand-dollar Vera Wang dress falls off her arms and to the floor. She turns kicks off her glass heels and runs to the bedroom to the biggest bed she ever seen in her life. Albre followed coming out of layers of clothes. When he reached the bedroom, he only had on socks and his manhood stood out nine inches in front of him. LaToya bounced on the bed in her bra and panties.

"So this how the President lives, um?" LaToya said as she motion for Albre to join her on the bed.

"I guess it is the Presidential Suite," Albre laughs as he bounces on the bed and starts lavishing kissing on LaToya. They were all over each other, kissing, licking, and sucking. It looks like they were wrestling in the big bed. Albre and LaToya make love three times that night and it was good. They were in love and happy.

CHAPTER 31

Graduation

Albre passes his final exam with flying colors, and graduated in the top ten percent of his class. His graduation was Kodak picture perfect. He walked across the stage in his Graduation gown to receive his diploma, as camera flashes. Graduation was held on a Tuesday, and everyone was in attendance. His dad and Janice, Cint, his grandmother, his brother, Supreme had flown down from Vegas. Shonta and his daughter, Bre was there. LaToya and her mom and to his surprise all of his friends were there. It was one of the proudest moments of his life, and everyone was so proud of him. He could have sworn he saw tears in his dad's eyes. The proudness was there without a doubt.

After graduation ceremony, everyone headed to his dad's house for a graduation celebration. Some of his classmates were there, and Albre was showered with gifts and congratulations.

After spending some time with his family, Albre went out front where all of his friends were standing around drinking and smoking.

"Here the Political Science major," said John.

"Yeah, that's me. Mr., I'm about to make some money in politics." Albre said jokingly.

"So now what?" Gage asked.

"Well, we'll see. But I have some idea what I'm gonna do," said Albre. "I just rather not go in to it right now."

"Man, you look real nerdy walking across that stage," said Ali playfully.

"And you had this damn fake a smile on your face. You looked like you had taken some acid and was having a smiling trip," Conan adds.

"Naw, for real," said Albre.

"Yeah, for real bro., wait until you see the video. I think we can sell that video," said John.

"I think we better hold on to it, for when he gets rich, black mail his ass," adds Gages and they all laugh.

"But we proud of you, my nigga," said John and the rest of his friends agree.

Albre felt good hearing that from his friends.

"So what are you gonna do tonight?" asked Conan.

"Man, I'm gonna chill with LaToya tonight. You know she graduates on Saturday," said Albre.

"LaToya's a good girl, Albre," said Gage.

"She's really great. I think I might marry her," said Albre.

"Man, you thinking about marriage already?" John said.

"Hell, nah man. I'm just saying I love that girl," said Albre.

"Sheeet, I was about to say, 'Damn, my nigga, you just graduated'," John laughs as he slaps Albre on the back.

"Hey, since I have you all here, I gonna let you know now. That this is my last summer in this game. So let's get some money. Ya'll in?" Albre asked.

"You know it, man," answers Gage.

"Hell, yeah," said Ali.

"I'm game," adds Conan.

"You know what, kid? I was thinking about the same thing. I'm tired of this shit, also," said John.

And that was their pact to make as much money as possible that summer.

CHAPTER 32

LaToya's Graduation Party and Gifts

LaToya graduation was held on a Saturday and she was glad to graduate from high school at the same time she was going to miss her classmates. They would be entering another stage in their lives and some she would remain in contact with and for those she wouldn't, she wishes them the best.

After her graduation ceremony, her mom had a graduation party at their apartment in Smiley Court. All LaToya's friends and family were there wishing her congratulations. Of course, Albre and his entourage were in company. LaToya receives a lot of gifts and was enjoying herself.

After the party, LaToya and Albre went back to his apartment in Vaughn Heights.

"Surprise, surprise," Albre tells LaToya as he gives her her graduation gift.

LaToya opens the envelope and finds a sixty thousand dollars check to the school of her choice. She had already been accepted in several universities such as UAB, Alabama State, Spellman, Tennessee, UCLA, and several other colleges.

"Thank you, Albre," said LaToya with tears in her eyes.

"Why are you crying?" Albre asked.

"Because I love you, I love you so very much," said LaToya.

"I love you, also," said Albre

Then he moves closer to her on the love seat. He also puts his arms around her and just holds her; and at that moment LaToya knew everything would be alright. She felt so honored to be Albre's girl. She promised to always do right by him.

CHAPTER 33

June was a Good Month

The month of June was a good month for Albre and his entourage. They made more money in that one month than they had during any other month. Southlawn, Smiley Court, Brickdale was jumping and Albre found himself going several nights without sleep.

Ali and Rick and Lil' Man didn't go back to court and all charges were dropped, thanks to Mr. Whitlock, their high-paid attorney. They had to pay the lawyer another ten thousand dollars to go along with the money Albre had given him as a retainer. However, Ali had cash in on the Roc. Albre was surprise when Ali told him how he had caught Roc coming out of a hotel down in Selma. Everyone knew the Roc had a mistress in Selma, so when Ali shows him the pictures and told him how it all went down and assures Albre that no one would ever find the body. The Roc had officially disappeared.

Albre gave Ali the fifty grand. The price he had placed on the Roc's head; and he highly respected Ali for stepping up to handle business. Albre liked Ali, because he was rough, smart, business-like, and a leader. He was sure Ali would reign the king over the Southside once Albre gladly gave up the throne. Everyone in their click knew Ali had killed the Roc. No one spoke a word of it. They respected and feared Ali. As for Ali, he was just fifty grand richer; and he couldn't wait to start pushing his own dope. As for Albre, everything was going well; no more, twenty percent to the Roc. They haven't seen any Narcos snooping around any of his traps or safehouse, and the money was pouring in like rain.

Cash had called Albre last week to inform him that Ku-Ting Won was coming to town and Albre were to meet at Top Knotch Jewelry at 6 p.m. Albre arrives at Top Knotch at 6:05 p.m. after stopping by his apartment to pick up three hundred grand. He planed on buying twenty bricks for fifteen grand apiece, the first time. Then the prices would drop to $12,750 a brick, and the dope was sure to be pure, well, and as pure as it gets in the United States, because this dope was coming straight off the waters from China.

"Hey, Jazz," said Albre.

"Hey, Albre. Go on back," said Jazz.

Then she pushes the button to let him through the counter, so he can go on back to Cash's office. She was cleaning some jewelry out front and there was no customers in the store. The door opens as Albre nears Cash's office and Cash signals him on in.

"Yo, Albre. Right on time," said Cash.

"Yeah, what's up?" Albre shakes Cash's hand and enters the office.

Cash closes the door. Everything in Cash's office is the usual.

"This my connect, Ku-Ting Won," Cash tells Albre.

"Mr. Won, this the young fella I've been telling you about and he's dying to meet you," continued Cash.

Albre greets the Asian and they shake hands.

"So now to business," said Mr. Won, "now, Albre, I can let you get this." He hands Albre a Ziploc bag full of cocaine. Albre can tell by the pinkish color that it's the real deal. However, he tests it anyway with some chemical he brought that turns blue when mixed with the cocaine. The bluer the better. "You like?" the Asian continues, "however, the first month prices will stay the same as when you was buying them from Cash."

Albre is satisfied after testing the dope. It's the bluest he had ever seen.

"But I thought it was gonna be fifteen grand apiece for the first transaction, and $12,750 afterwards," said Albre with confusion.

"Maybe you heard me wrong," interrupts Cash.

"This quality of cocaine, Mr. Albre, I wouldn't complain. Besides, business is business," said Mr. Won.

With this quality of dope, Albre was sure he could step on it and get 26 or 27 kilos and still have the best dope in the Gump.

"Okay, that's cool, Mr. Won," Albre tells him.

The Asian asked, "You have the money?"

"It's all there, but count it if you want," said Albre.

Then he sets the suitcase with the 300 hundred grand down on Cash's desk and opens it.

"Three hundred grand," said the Asian.

"Yeah, some bulls might be wrinkle," said Albre and smiles.

"Drug money, I wouldn't expect anything different; and I don't have to count it. I can weigh it," said Mr. Won with a grin on his face. He closed the suitcase and picks it up as if weighing it.

Albre no doubt, don't think he's joking. Surely, Mr. Won has handled enough money that he probably could weigh it right down to the dollar.

"Here's the key, Mr. Albre," said the Asian, "there's a van parked a block over on Goode Street. It's white with tinted window. You can't miss it."

"Thank you, and nice doing business with you," said Albre as he accepts the keys to the van.

"I'll call you later," said Cash as Albre walks out the office.

"Yeah, we'll be in touch and Mr. Won, have a good day," said Albre.

When Albre gets back in his truck, he thinks to himself, something didn't smell right about the Asian guy. But he was too busy thinking of the money he would make with this uncut dope. He pushes the previous thought from his mind then he goes to pick up Ali to get the van and trail him to the E-Z storage, not the one he and Cash use in Shorter. But to an E-Z storage in Prattville. Once they parked the van in the E-Z storage and on the way back to Montgomery, Albre and Ali have a long conversation.

Albre tells Ali that he's about to get out the game and he wanted him close, so he could learn what he didn't know. He wanted to teach Ali everything about the dope game. Albre said he would show him how to hide money. Always cover his rearview mirror to make sure he wasn't being followed and the such; because he wants him to take over because he didn't trust Gage anymore. Gage was addicted to the cocaine and would soon fall.

CHAPTER 34

July...Things Were Good

Albre was sitting in Brickdale. Gage had just got back from picking up money from all the traps and Albre had already counted 135 thousand and still had the money from Brickdale to count.

Things were good. The new dope was a hit. Albre step on the twenty kilos and got 27 kilos. Cint had cooked up most of it, and the rest they sold in soft. Cint was cooking dope all the time now. She had lost about thirty pounds and looked rough. Albre had given up hope on her. Because he was too far-gone. Gage face was shrinking from all the cocaine he snorted daily. John was gone out of town all the time on business. Ali was in Smiley Court at Cint's apartment. The spot that was making the most money. Rick was in Smiley Court with Ali. Conan, Lil' Man and Lil' Troy were all in Southlawn.

"Hello?" Albre answers his cell.

"Hey. Where you at?" Shonta asked. She was his baby's momma.

"Trapping," Albre tells her.

"Well, I was wondering what you gonna be doing tomorrow. Could you pick Bre up from Girl Scout?" Shonta asked.

"Yeah, what time?" Albre asked.

"Around three," said Shonta.

"Aight, you straight. You sure that's all you want?" Albre asked.

"Yeah, I'm just worried about you. I had this dream about you got killed," said Shonta.

Oh, here she goes with this dream shit again, Albre thought.

"Well, when I die, I'm gonna take 10 niggas with me," jokes Albre trying to make lightly as he quotes a rap song.

"Just be careful, okay? I love you," Shonta tells him.

"I love you, too, Shonta," reponds Albre.

Then he hangs up his cell phone and continues to count the money. When he finished, he got a total of 260 thousand dollars. He would take two hundred thousand and re-up tomorrow and he would take the sixty grand and places with the 420 grand he had in his apartment. He had to make another trip to his safe deposit box in Atlanta before the week was out. He calls Ali.

"What's up, Albre?" Ali said recognizing the number on the caller ID.

"Shit, I'm going to Atlanta on Friday to buy me a ride. Want to come along?" Albre asked him.

"Hell, yeah. I need to buy me some new wheels, also," replied Ali.

"Well, bring some cash. I'll holla at you later; and don't tell anyone where you going, aight?" Albre said and hung up the phone.

The next day Albre picks up his daughter, Bre, from Girl Scouts.

"Hey, Daddy," said Bre as she climbs up in the back seat of Albre's Suburban.

"Hey, sweetheart; put on your seatbelt," Albre tells his daughter then asks, "how was Girl Scouts?

"We had fun, I learned how to make brownies," said Bre, "want me to show you?"

"Not today, baby. Daddy's kinda busy," said Albre.

He looks into his rearview mirror to see the sad expression on his daughter's face. He felt guilty for not spending much time with her lately. But he promised himself he would make it up to her when this was all over.

Albre drops his daughter off at his grandma's house, and head to his apartment being sure he's not followed. Then he gets the money from his apartment and heads to Top Knotch.

"Well, nice to see you again," said Mr. Won, the Asian tells him as they closed the door.

Cash was sitting behind his desk as usual.

"What's up, Cash?" Albre asked.

"Oh, you know business as usual," replies Cash.

"Here's the money," Albre tells the Asian.

This time Mr. Won doesn't even open it to look inside he just give the keys to a van and tells him where it's parked.

"Ya'll have a good one." said Albre.

Albre leaves, not for small talk. He doesn't want to be friendly with the Asian. Straight business because he knows the Asian is part of the notorious Asian mafia he had heard so much about and most of their friends winds up dead. Albre picks up Ali and has Ali get the van and trail him to an E-Z storage in Prattville.

CHAPTER 35

Albre and Ali are Robbed

Albre leaves his apartment with 480 thousand dollars. He left LaToya at the apartment only telling her that he was going to Atlanta. He had twenty thousand dollars separate so he could add it to the value of his truck, which he planned to trade in because he was recognized in the Gump.

Albre picks Ali up from Cint's apartment in Smiley Court when he pulls up in front of the apartment, Ali sees his truck and gets in with a paper bag. Albre assumes it's money.

"Yo, Albre," said Ali as he greets him as he gets in.

"What's up, Ali?" said Albre.

"I brought thirty grand, you think that's will cop me something nice," said Ali.

"No doubt, I bet my man at Mad Cars got something for you," Albre tells him. He puts the truck in drive and heads towards I-85.

"Man, in a couple of weeks, I'm gonna bounce," Albre tells Ali.

"You know where you going?" Ali asked.

"I got some ideas, but it far away from here," said Albre.

"I bet you made enough money this last year to have you set for life," said Ali.

"Yeah, the money good. But it ain't 'bout the money for me. I don't want to live the rest of my life looking over my shoulder, worried about who's trying to sell on my side, looking out the window to make sure ain't no Narcos nearby, you know what I'm saying?" Albre asked him.

"Yeah, I guess," replies Ali.

Albre knows Ali doesn't understand because he grew up in the streets and the streets he knows.

"See, I want the same thing you want in life. You know, nice rides, big houses, fine hoes, and expensive clothes. Except I don't want to be looking over my shoulder worrying about going to jail, or getting killed," said Albre, "you know we all got to have goals, and mine was to finish college and start my own business. Now that I have finished college, and all this money I got saved. Here my chance to get out the game."

"Once in the game always in the game," responded Ali.

"How true; but a different game. Don't get me wrong. I'm gonna miss it and I had some fun, my nigga. But the funs not over, Shidd, when I get where I'm going. You can come out and I'll show you different things, my nigga. Because it's more to life than what you see in the Gump," said Albre.

"You right, my nigga, I went to Cancun once and man, I loved that place. Wish I could have stayed," said Ali.

"You can," said Albre as he smiles, letting everything he said to Ali soak in. But out of everyone, he knew Ali was just like him. Only he had more doors open to him than Ali did, "why don't you go to college?"

"Hell, I ain't even finished high school," said Ali.

"Get your GED. It's just as good, and you can still go to college. College life is good," said Albre as he noticed the gas light came on, "damn, we got to stop and get some gas." Albre pulled off on an exit in Phoenix City, Alabama.

But to their surprise, it was a brown Acura following them driven by Scoopy and Powell. They had been following them since they left Smiley Court. They were so busy talking that neither Albre nor Ali looked back to see that they were being followed.

"They're pulling off on the exit to Phoenix City," Scoopy told Powell who was driving.

"I see 'em," said Powell slowing down as not to be seen by the passenger of the Suburban.

Powell and Scoopy had parked on the far side of the Exxon. Before they got out, they had on their black fitted caps and a blue bandana around their faces. Powell and Scoopy came out of nowhere. Powell draws a 9mm Smith & Wesson on Ali and Scoopy hold a .45 on Albre. Albre looks up in surprise, not having time to grab his Glock .40 from under the seat.

"Get out the truck, bitch," yells Scoopy at Albre.

Albre steps out the truck, knowing the procedure with his hands in the air.

"What the fuck is in your pocket, mother fucker?" Powell screams at Ali while he frisks him. Scoopy does the same to Albre.

"Where's the money at, mother fucker?" said Scoopy.

"That's all the money we got," said Albre referring to the money they had taken out of their pockets.

"That's bullshit," said Scoopy.

He hits Albre on the side of the head with the butt of the 45. Then Powell follows suit and hits Ali with the butt of his pistol. But, Ali had braced himself for the impact. However, he still went down to the ground. Powell jumps in Albre's truck. Scoopy runs back to where their car was parked, and before Albre and Ali could get up to get help, the robbers were gone.

"Damn," Albre cursed them.

"Who the fuck? What the fuck?" Ali was saying.

"That's them niggas I seen following me a couple of months ago. Damn, I can't believe I slip like that and not watching my back," said Albre.

"How the fuck we gonna get him," said Ali.

"Shit," said Albre mad as fuck, "let's go call somebody to come get us." Albre and Ali both left their cell phones in the truck.

Albre and Ali went inside the store and told the clerk what happened. The clerk was this old white man.

"Hey, can we use your phone?" asked Albre, "we just got robbed and they stole our truck."

"Yeah, I seen it happen; I already called the police. They should be on their way," said the white man.

"Alright, now can I use your phone?" Albre asked again. God, he forgot he had to report his truck stolen to collect his insurance benefits. Too bad the money wasn't insured.

"Here you go," said the white guy, passing Albre a cordless phone.

"Thanks," replied Albre.

He calls several numbers. He couldn't reach Gage or John. Finally, he called LaToya and told her where he was and that someone stole his truck, not daring to say anything about the money in front of the clerk. By the time he got off the phone with LaToya, the Phoenix police had arrived at the gas station. Albre and Ali gave them the rundown of what had happened leaving out the details of the money they had inside the truck.

"Where ya'll from?" said one of the two red neck cops whose name tag identified him as Sgt. Foley.

"We from Montgomery," responded Ali.

"Uh huh, and where were ya'll going?" Sgt. Foley asked as the other officer whose nametag was Officer Wright took down their addresses and other information in the police report.

"We were going to Atlanta, sir," said Albre.

"Business or pleasure?" Sgt. Foley asked.

"A little of both," said Albre matter of factly.

"Okay, describe the truck again," said Sgt. Foley eying Albre and Ali suspiciously.

"It was a butter scotch candy '89 Chevy Suburban. Like the candy that you eat. It had 22" Chrome Spreewell rims," said Albre.

"And how did you pay for it?" Sgt. Foley asked.

"Does it matter how I paid for it? It was insured," said Albre snapping.

"Um huh," said Sgt. Foley.

"Go ask the clerk if they have video coverage of the gas pump?" Sgt. Foley told Officer Wright.

After a couple of seconds later, Officer Wright returns and told him they did not.

"Well, let us get a statement from the clerk, and we'll need to take you guys down to the police station to finish the police report," Sgt. Foley told them.

"Whatever, officer," said Albre.

He could tell Ali was irritated also. But Ali kept his mouth closed and openly answered only the questions asked of him. They were at the police station three hours before LaToya arrives in the Lexus Albre had bought for her.

"Baby, ya'll alright?" LaToya asked as they got into the car.

"We good. Hell, these damn cops acting like we did something wrong. We the ones who got robbed," said Albre.

"Mother fucking redneck," said Ali, "damn, man...them mother fuckers took the money I had saved to get me a nice ride. Shit, I got some more money, but when I find out who them niggas was, they ass gonna pay." Albre didn't doubt Ali for not one second.

"I think them was the same guys that was following us that day we went to the movies," Albre told LaToya.

"I remember. The one in the white Lexus," said LaToya.

"Yeah, but they was in another car," said Albre.

"A 1994 Acura Legend. Black," said Ali.

"Damn, I had a half million dollars in that truck. I was gonna drop it off at the bank in Atlanta," said Albre more to himself than the others.

LaToya's and Ali's mouth dropped out in awe.

CHAPTER 36

The Day after the Robbery

The following day, everyone had heard of Albre and Ali getting robbed. There was rumor of different amount of money that had gotten taken; some said half a million and some said a million dollars. That night after the robbery, Albre had a talk with LaToya and told her that it was over with for him and the dope game. LaToya understood. He said he had a couple more things to take care of then he was leaving Montgomery. He asked her did she want to go with him and she said she did.

"Where you gonna go?" LaToya asked him that night.

"I don't know yet," confided Albre.

"But I'm thinking Los Angeles," he said.

"I think I would love Los Angeles. Then I would go to school at UCLA," said LaToya.

"Then Los Angeles it is," said Albre.

He told her to go ahead and accept UCLA, to send her tuition check, and not to tell anyone not even her mom. They would call her once they got there.

While Albre was sitting in Brickdale waiting on John to come by, he rolled him a nice blunt of Hydro.

"Say, Cint," said Albre.

"Yeah," replied Cint from the back of the room.

"Call Ali and find out how much dope he got left," said Albre.

"Aight, give me five minutes," said Cint.

And right before John arrived, Cint told him Ali said that he had three kilos of crack in Smiley Court. Conan had two and a half in Southlawn and eight ounces of cocaine.

"What's up, Albre?" John asked.

"Damn, man. You sure know how to get ghost," Albre tells him.

"Business, I was gone on a business trip," said John, "I heard that you and Ali got robbed," he continued, "yeah, let's take a ride man.

We need to talk," Albre told him and John looked surprised wondering what that was about.

Albre was back driving his Cutlass until the first of August. Once the insurance company investigated, they would cut him a check to replace his truck. His insurance agent said his truck was valued at twenty-six thousand dollars, which was less than he put in the truck. But was okay by him. Instead, they took John Impala out for a ride, once they were out of Brickdale, Albre fired up another blunt of Hydro.

"Say, John, you know I love you, man," said Albre between puffs.

"I love you, too, bro," said John.

Albre looked over at John and waited for Albre's eyes to meet his.

"It's over with, man. I'm leaving on the first of the month," said Albre which was two weeks away.

"Where you gonna go? And what you gonna do?" John asked.

"I can't say where I'm going right now. But LaToya is going with me," said Albre.

"How much money you got robbed for. You alright?" John asked.

"They got me for a half a million. I knew I shouldn't have had that much money on me. But I was going to drop it off. However, I'm straight.

I got a little money saved," said Albre.

He said little money, in actuality; he had over three million dollars saved.

"So I guess this is it, huh?" John asked.

"Yeah, this it. But it's not the end, man. You know you like a little brother to me, so I'll always be there when and if you need me. Just a phone a way," said Albre.

By that time, John had reached Lowndes County driving the back way to avoid the heavy traffic and the State Troopers. So when they reached a little town called White Hall, John stops at a Park that located on the Alabama River called Holy Ground. It was an actual battlefield back in the days. They got out and observed the environment, which was beautiful. They talked and smoked some more blunts for about an hour. Then they drove back to Montgomery.

Once they reached Brickdale, and before Albre got out the car, John said, "I know we gonna hang out this weekend."

"You better believe it," said Albre.

"And everything on me, man. Party at the Rose," said John.

"Aight, love you, man," said Albre as he got out.

"Love you, too, man," said John. Then he was off. Albre could see exhaust coming from the Chevy tail pipe of the Impala.

CHAPTER 37

The Rose

The Rose was the spot for Saturday night. LaToya was hanging out with her girlfriends in her Lexus. Albre was also having the time of his life with his click. Everything that was anybody was at the Rose; and Mystikal was performing. The Rose is a club in a class all by itself. When you come to Montgomery, you had to go to The Rose. It was a formal wear club. So Albre was dressed to impress in his Calvin Klein too large button up shirt. A pair of Stacy's Adam boots, and his dread freshly twisted.

John was dressed to par also in a purple on purple Sean John outfit; and everyone else was exceptionally dressed as they sat upstairs in the MIP section. With the perfect view that looked down on the entire club. There were other VIP rooms in the club. But nothing even compare to the MVP room which you usually had to reserve a couple of months early for the price of five grand. That's just for the room. The Rose was a two-drink mini club. But the VIP's and MVP rooms were a two setup minimum. Drinks run you about ten dollars. But the setup was two hundred dollars or more. That includes a bottle of champagne or Cognac, your choice, and a case of beer.

The MVP room was a circular room with green walls. White leather horseshoe shape sofa. A phone directly linked to the manager's office and three waitresses of your own.

Albre, John, Ali, Conan, Gage, Rick, Lil' Man and Lil' Troy were all enjoying themselves. A host of girls were crowding about the room and a club full of girls trying to get in the MVP room whenever they could, because they knew it was some ballers in there. The bouncers at the door kept out all unwanted guests.

"This shit the bomb," said Lil' Troy the youngest of the group. This was his first time in the MVP room of The Rose.

"Hell, yeah," someone else said.

"Damn, it ain't enough girls in here," said Ali and John to the bouncer to let some more girls in.

The phone rings and it can't be anyone but the manager. Since the phone is directly linked to his office.

John answers, "Hey, ya'll straight up there?" J.J. asked.

J.J. was the owner of the club. The manager was a broad named Cady.

"Yeah, we good," said John.

"Well, I'm sending a set-up up there on the house," said J.J. He only said those words when someone was spending big money; and they were most definitely spending a working man salary tonight.

"Aight, Remy," said John in between puff of the blunts.

"That was J.J. He know we spending money, he wants us to spend some more," John tells them and pulls out a wad of hundred dollar bills and wave them in the air. The strippers were all over John trying to get that money.

Albre was high as hell, drunk out of his mind but he was having a good time, getting a lap dance from this stripper named Cherry.

"Do the thunder clap," Albre tells Cherry.

She makes her ass clap you can hear it clack, clack, clack! And Albre smiles.

Mystikal is heard over the speakers singing, "Shake it, shake it, shake that ass..."

They partied until the wee hours of the morning. J.J. had his limousine take them home because nobody was able to drive.

CHAPTER 38

Albre Tells Shonta and Bre That He's Moving

The following week after Albre was running around taking care of all his lose ends, he had dropped by and told his baby momma, Shonta that he was moving, and he would call her when he gets where he's going.

"Damn, Albre, why you ain't tell me sooner?" Shonta asked him.

"Because I just decided, Shonta. Don't worry about anything. You know I love you and Bre and I'm always gonna take care of ya'll," said Albre.

"That's not the point, Albre," said Shonta

Then she started to cry, and then his daughter started to cry; not really understand what was going on, only that her mom was crying.

"Baby girl, don't cry. Daddy loves you," said Albre to his daughter. He knew this was going to be the hardest part.

"I love you, too, Daddy," said Bre as she stopped crying.

"You be a good girl, okay?" Albre said.

"I will, Daddy," said Bre as his daughter hugs him.

"Shonta, I love you, okay. Once I get settled, you and Bre can come if you want," said Albre.

"Albre, I understand. You got to go on with your life. I'm just gonna miss you, that's all. I'm good. We'll be alright. Just promise me you will be careful, okay?" Shonta said.

"I will. I'll be in touch soon, okay? I love you," said Albre. Then he kisses Shonta on the lips.

"I love you, too, princess," said Albre to his daughter.

"I love you, Daddy," said his daughter.

"I love you, too, Albre," said Shonta.

Albre leaves Shonta's apartment feeling heart broken. But he knows it's something he must do. He goes by his dad's house in Ridgecrest.

Albre tells his dad who's out back cleaning his boat, "Daddy, I'm leaving next week."

Dad loves that boat, Albre thinks to himself, probably more than me.

His dad looks up and says, "And where do you think you're going?"

His dad said those words in a tone Albre only heard once in his life.

"Well, me and LaToya are moving to Los Angeles," said Albre.

"When you decided this?" asked his dad. Albre had his full attention now.

"Well, I've been thinking about it. But I guess I made up my mind after I got robbed," said Albre.

Then his dad asked, "You got robbed, boy? Why didn't you tell me you got robbed?"

"About two weeks ago. They took my truck and some money. Me and a friend was going to Atlanta. They robbed us at a gas station in Phoenix City," said Albre. His dad thinks him and his son don't communicate anymore.

"Why didn't you tell me, son? Have the police figured out who it was?" his dad asked him.

"Nah, the police don't know, and I ain't want you worried, dad," said Albre.

"I worry about you being in those streets. I guess it's best that you are leaving before you end up dead or in prison," his dad said. Then as soon as he said those words, he regretted it. Because he knew Albre was too smart to follow his footsteps.

"So what are you gonna do in California?" he asked him.

"I'm gonna settle down first then I'm gonna open me a management company," Albre continued, "LaToya, she's going to go to school at UCLA."

"Well, I don't know what to say, son..." he pauses, "you know I love you, and I wish you the best." He looks Albre in the eye.

"I know, Dad. I love you, too," said Albre.

"Is there anything me and Janice can do for you?" he asked him. Janice was his dad's girlfriend and Albre was going to stop by her house next and tell her good bye in person.

"Thanks pop. But I'm straight. I got a little money saved up," he tells his dad.

"Well, you go by there and tell Janice. She gonna be surprised. But she loves you, too," his dad said.

He hugs his father. "I love you, Dad. I'm gonna miss you, man," said Albre as tears escape.

"I know, son. Just be careful, okay?" he tells Albre.

Albre turns to leave and his dad tells him, "Boy, you know you can't run from your problems, so if you gotten into something stay and face it like a man."

"Nah, pops, I'm just tired of the game. I'm tired of Montgomery," said Albre and left.

His dad shakes his head, glad that his son is turning out to be the man he knew he was. No doubt in his mind that Albre would be successful in anything he wanted to do. He was a leader. After Albre stops by Janice's house. He goes to Brickdale where he meets Ali, Conan, Gage, Cint is there also.

"Hey, look guys, I just wanted to let you guys know that I'm leaving town for a while, and Ali's the man," Albre tells the group and Gage looks at him suspiciously.

"Damn, Albre that's fucked up man. I've been with you from day one," said Gage in anger.

"And you know what? You're right. But you snort too fucking much powder, nigga," said Albre.

Everyone looks at him because they don't know what to expect. But they all knew he was right even Cint was nodding her head in agreement.

"Who the fuck are you to say I snort too much powder? I can do what the fuck I want," said Gage and stood up.

"Sit your ass down, nigga. What you gonna do? Swing on me? Besides I told you a minute ago to slack up on the powder. We might snort as a recreation, but you got carried away. That's why I don't snort no more. The number one rule. Don't get high on your own supply," said Albre and Gage obediently sits down then Albre continues, "now, you can do your thing. But I said I'm leaving Ali to run thing as he sees fit."

"Why Ali?" asked Conan.

"Because of what he showed me, you got a problem with that?" Albre was all in Conan's face now because Gage had his blood boiling.

"Naw, man. I'm cool with that. Shidd Ali, my nigga," replied Conan.

"Chill out, Albre," said Ali trying to calm Albre down.

"Look, I don't want to be no boss. I want us all to make money. You can make money with me or on your own. But I got Albre's connect," said Ali and pauses for effect. "I love all ya'll niggas so why ya'll tripping on me?"

"We ain't tripping, Ali," said Conan.

"Where are you going, Albre?" Cint asked trying to change the subject.

Gage was boiling; it got to him more than Albre thought. He knew it would be animosity. Albre just hope it blew over.

"I can't say right now. But I just wanted to let ya'll know next week I'm out. I got to take care of some business," said Albre.

"Shidd, you probably running cause ya'll scary ass got robbed," said Gage.

This nigga must be high right now, Albre thinks. Where else does he get this courage from?

"Look, I'm tired of your motherfucking shit, Gage," Ali was telling him. "we know ya'll bitch ass been stealing, because your stash always short. The only reason you still here, still breathing because I told Albre you was stressing."

"Know what? Fuck ya'll. Fuck ya'll niggas," said Gage said and stormed out the door. Ali was on his heels out the door. But, Albre stops him.

"Let him go," said Albre.

"Cint, you good?" Albre said.

"I'm gonna miss you," said Cint and started crying.

"Ah, bitch, you gonna miss the dope," said Albre.

"Stop crying, trying to suck me up. Hell, I'm gonna miss ya'll, too. But, I'll be back and I'm gonna come with some money for you. I know I'm gonna spend it on dope," said Albre.

"No, I'm not. I'm gonna get cleaned," said Cint, "you'll see when you get back. You'll see."

"Well, I hope you do. Try for me, alright?" Albre said as he counted out five grand and gave it to Cint.

"Hey, I love you, too. Be good," he said and gave Cint a hug.

"So what now, player?" Conan asked him.

"Don't let my absence stop nothing," Albre tells him and gives him some daps.

"Well, this is it, my nigga," said Ali.

"Yep. The end of chapter one," Albre smiles and Ali laughs.

"Hey, walk me out to my car, Ali," Albre tells him.

"Later, ya'll," he tells Cint and Conan.

And they wish him farewell on his trip which they both knew he wasn't coming back.

"What's up?" Ali asked as him and Albre stand by Albre's Cutlass.

"I know you bout that dough," said Albre.

"Yeah," Ali answered.

"Too bad, it's up to you now," Albre laughs and gets in his car.

"Fuck, I know it ain't like that," said Ali leaning in the passenger window.

"Naw, man. I'm just playing. Holla at John. He got some in for ya," said Albre.

"What about that cat from Florida you had hook up with?" Ali asked.

"They dirty, Ali. Something ain't right about him and Cash. Take my word for it man. Stay away from them two," Albre tells him. Albre still hasn't put his finger on what it was about Cash and the Asian. But he was going find out because he had one last transaction to make with them before he left.

"Later," said Albre as he left Brickdale for the last time.

"Later, man," Ali tells him.

He returns to his apartment to find LaToya there. They were going to spend the last week in a hotel so everything he wasn't giving to Goodwill was packed in boxes. LaToya had been busy also tying up loose ends. She had told her mom that she was going away with Albre. But she didn't know where yet, and she would call her as soon as she knew. Her mom was worried. However, she assures her that she would be okay and gave her the money. Albre told her to give her mother money for the car that she was trying to get. When she opened the brown paper bag, LaToya told her it was from Albre. Her mother cried and cried. LaToya said goodbye to her brothers and sisters, and left her mother in tears. She was so emotional.

That night LaToya and Albre enjoy each other's company. LaToya wanted to have sex, but Albre wasn't up to it, besides his mind was racing.

"I love you, baby," said Albre.

"I love you, too, baby," replied LaToya.

"Better days, better days," said Albre as he held her and went to sleep.

CHAPTER 39

Meeting at Top Knotch Jewelry Store

Albre was scheduled to meet Mr. Won and Cash at Top Knotch Jewelry at 7 p.m. The jewelry store closed at 6 p.m. He was driving a brand new Black Mercedes 500. The insurance company had cut him a check for twenty-five grand; and he added fourteen more from the sale of the Cutlass, which he got fifteen grand. Also, the sale of LaToya's Lexus which he got thirty-seven grand for which was damn near the value of the car because it wasn't even a couple of months old.

He had left LaToya at the hotel. When he arrived at Top Knotch Jewelry; he pulls his Glock 9 from under the seat, and gets his bag out the back seat with the money in it. He goes inside but he doesn't see anyone at the front counter which isn't usual since it was seven o'clock. Jazz probably was gone for the day. He goes on to the back when he goes through the counter door it make a short buzz sound that would signal Cash in his office that he was there. Albre goes back to the office. He hears voices, but as he gets closer, the office's door is cracked and the voices he realizes is a radio. He pushes the door open and the scene shocks him.

Cash was leaning over his desk with his head on the desk. You could see the hole in his head from a gunshot. The Asian, Mr. Won, was sprawled on the floor with a pool of blood under him; and two other guys, one in the chair with several holes in his chest. Albre recognizes him as Charles, Cash muscle man. The other was folded up in the corner as if he had been struggling with someone. Albre didn't see a hold in him as he was clearly dead and blood ran out his nose and ears. He recognized this dude from seeing him with Mr. Won. He was the Asian's bodyguard.

Albre took in the rest of the office. The two safes Cash had in his office where he kept the expensive jewelry was opened and emptied. However, when he came in he remembers seeing jewelry in the counter out front. That was the least expensive jewelry.

Albre gathers himself and went to thinking logically. He checked the file cabinet where Cash kept the monitor and video cassettes of the store. He grabs the tape. Then found and old towel in the trash can beside Cash's desk. He wipes down everything he touched: doorknobs, everything. Then he puts the tape inside his bag and exited the store as fast as he could.

When he got back to the hotel room. He told LaToya to change their flight plans and get them the first flight she could to Los Angeles.

"What's up, baby? Why you in such a hurry?" LaToya asked.

"Just make those flight arranged. Pay extra expenses with your credit card and pack our bags," said Albre.

LaToya calls and confirms a flight leaving at 11:45 p.m. from Montgomery international airport.

"I got us a flight leaving Montgomery international at 11:45 p.m. with one hour layover in Atlanta," said LaToya.

"Good, I'll be back in a minute," said Albre.

He took the Mercedes he had just bought over to Janice's house and parked it in her garage. His father was over at Janice when he got there. He told his dad what happened at Top Knotch and that the tape along with 200 thousand dollars was in the trunk of the car. His dad said he would take care of the car and put the tape and money up.

Albre caught a taxi back to the hotel room. It was 9:50 p.m. when he got there.

"Call a taxi and be ready to leave when I get out the shower," he tells LaToya.

"Okay, baby," said LaToya as she calls a taxi.

LaToya was watching the news while Albre was in the shower, and the woman in the news was talking about the robbery of Top Knotch Jewelry; four people were dead, and a black Mercedes 500 was seen leaving the scene of the crime.

"Oh my gawd," said LaToya to herself.

"Police believe that at least 3.5 million in cash and jewelry was taken and an unknown amount of drugs," said the news reporter.

"I know Albre didn't just pull that robbery off," said LaToya, "that's why he's in such a hurry."

She turns the TV off and wonders how did Albre pulled that off. But she knew better than to ask. Albre comes out the shower and they exited the hotel room into the awaiting cab.

EPILOGUE

Albre and LaToya had been in Los Angeles for two weeks now; and everything was going beautifully. Albre looked stress-free. They had an apartment on Sunset Boulevard and they were driving two rental cars.

LaToya had went and signed up for classes at UCLA and started the following week.

Albre was looking for a home they could afford. He had already located an office building that he was going to lease for his business. They were more than comfortable. Albre had a little under three million dollars left. That was still in the safe deposit in Atlanta. He had to drive down and get it soon. After he had told LaToya, what happened at Top Knotch Jewelry on the plane to Los Angeles and she was relieved that he didn't do it.

His dad had sent the money and tape to Los Angeles with a friend who had a private jet, and he had sold the car and mailed Albre the money from that check.

Albre and LaToya sat watching the video footage of the tape from Top Knotch Jewelry. It only showed the front of the store. You could see who entered and left. As they continued watching the tape, they see two guys coming in the store with ski masks on. They were moving fast straight to the back of the store and a short period of time lapse they exited the store.

"Damn, that guy walks like Gage," said LaToya.

Albre pauses the tape, and sure enough, it was Gage; and he had on the Mark Jacob watch. Albre gave him on his birthday.

"Who's that guy with him?" LaToya asked.

"Hell, I have no idea," said Albre and truly he didn't.

He had enough on his plate to worry about it. He would keep that tape, in case the scene he witness at Top Knotch Jewelry ever came back to haunt him.

"I didn't think he had it in him," Albre tells LaToya.

"He looks desperate," replied LaToya so innocently.

She just doesn't know how right she was. Desperate indeed.

TO BE CONTINUED...

ABOUT THE AUTHOR

Bo Hall

He is a native of Montgomery, AL and writes under his pen name Bo Hall. He is currently incarcerated in Georgia and is hard at work on his second street novel of the "Days of My Life Series." And he hopes to make parole.

He would love to hear from you and your feedback. He can be reached on Facebook and Twitter, at https://www.facebook.com/bohall83 and www.twitter.com/bohall83